Hijack

Wendy Cartmell

Costa Press

Copyright © Wendy Cartmell 2015
Published by Costa Press
ISBN-13: 978-1502309839
ISBN-10: 1502309831
Wendy Cartmell has asserted her right under the Copyright Designs and Patents Act 1998 to be identified as the author of this work.
All characters and events in this publication, other than those in the public domain, are fictitious and any resemblance to real persons, living or dead is purely coincidental.

Prologue
Bagram Detention Centre
Afghanistan

The young man swung from a rope tied around his hands and attached to a metal hook in the ceiling. He'd been up there for five hours. Luckily he'd died after three. His poor tortured and abused body no longer able to take the punishment meted out by the soldiers.

The naked light bulb in the cell was burning, as it had done since the boy's arrival at the detention centre several months earlier, harshly illuminating the bare concrete walls, ceiling and floor. There had been no respite from the light. Nor from the shouting of the soldiers as they tortured other prisoners in the block.

Although he had been young and strong when grabbed from the garage by the coalition forces, where he was working on a Land Rover that refused to start, it hadn't saved him. For some reason the soldiers seemed to think he was part of an illegal militia, not a simple motor mechanic. No matter what he'd said, how long and hard he'd screamed or whimpered and cried, they'd ignored his distress and continued with the beatings and interrogations.

Being fed on the occasional chunk of bread and jug of water pushed contemptuously into his cell, had meant his body soon turned against him, burning up fat and muscle in the absence of the fuel it needed to survive. Daily and nightly attacks from fists, batons and worse, had worn out his wasted body, until one by one his internal organs shut down.

The last to go was his heart. As it beat its final tattoo the boy's thoughts were for his family. Did they know where he was? Would they be told he'd died? Would his brother, Kourash, thousands of miles away in England hear of his fate?

With his last breath he whispered his father's name.....

Day 1
09:55 hours

He'd known there was something wrong the minute he saw them through the window. The innocuous group of cyclists waiting to board the train at Dent railway station. It wasn't because they were sweating, although the day was sunny but cold. It wasn't even that they were looking nervously around, their eyes always going back to the tallest young man in the middle of their huddled group, as if seeking reassurance. Nor the fact that as soon as the train juddered to a stop at the platform they immediately split up, boarding the train in two groups. One group to each of the two carriages, instead of staying together. It wasn't those things individually. But put them together? Well that was a cause for concern.

As this was happening, Sgt Billy Williams was on the phone to his boss, Sgt Major Crane. Billy had rung him to confirm he'd be at Aldershot Garrison later that day, reporting back to Provost Barracks, the home of the Special Investigations Branch of the Royal Military Police. Billy was taking the scenic train route, from Carlisle to Settle on the return journey from his parent's house in Carlisle, where he'd spent the weekend.

Billy watched with interest the young men who boarded the carriage. One boy took off the scarf he was wearing around his neck, revealing two sturdy bicycle chains with locks on. He took them from around his neck and passed one to his fellow traveller. The young man tethered his bike to the pole by the carriage entrance, as did his companion. Why would you chain your bike to the pole if you were staying in the carriage, Billy wondered. Were they that distrustful of people? Or was there an ulterior motive? Once the bikes were chained up, the two young men seemed unable to keep still. Hands wringing. Brows sweating. Teeth chewing lips. It made Billy nervous just watching them. With a suspicious frown, he looked out of the window. The train was approaching the Ribble Viaduct, a 100 ft high structure with 24 arches. A remote construction set high up on the Yorkshire Dales and now a popular tourist attraction. The viaduct had been built in the 1800's by hundreds of Irish navvies who lived and worked on the construction site. But there were no shanty towns still standing. All trace of the workers had been wiped from the face of the barren earth and the Dales returned to their majestic, isolated, glory.

As one of the cyclists moved to stand close to the emergency stop cord, Billy said into his mobile phone, "Boss, I think there's a problem with the Carlisle to Settle train." He was going to add - I think the shit's just about to hit the fan - when it well and truly did. The cyclist reached for the emergency cord and yanked it.

So with the cool calm reactions ingrained in him from his military training, Billy said instead, "Possible hijack situation. The train's stopping in the middle of the Ribble Viaduct. Estimate at least six hijackers, cyclists who boarded the train at Dent. Will report back when I know more."

But his calm, quick reactions didn't stop him feeling apprehensive. Fear wriggled like a worm through his veins. A purveyor of bad news. With worse to come, no doubt.

Billy had instinctively risen from his seat during the conversation and holding the seat backs, using them to keep his balance during the sharp reduction in the speed of the train, he made his way to the toilet. He was talking to Crane via the hands-free mobile phone cord that ran from his ear to his phone, which was hidden from view in the pocket of his brown leather jacket.

With the door closed, the smell of the chemical toilet was strong in the small space and he breathed through his mouth in an effort to minimise it. Cutting the call and then turning off the volume on his mobile, he looked around the tiny cubicle. All the surfaces were stainless steel and the small space seemed coffin-like and claustrophobic. The walls were pre-fabricated and moulded, with no cracks or gaps in them that he could utilise. Bugger. He needed a hiding place and he needed it now. There would only be a few moment's grace before he was found. Then he spotted a small cupboard built into the wall underneath the sink. Squatting down and grasping the handle, Billy was relieved to find the cupboard unlocked. He popped his phone inside and plugged the cord, which was still dangling from his ear, into his iPod instead. Straightening up he pushed open the door and backed out of the toilet. Slap bang into the barrel of a revolver. A small smile played across Billy's lips. The game was on.

10:00 hours

"Go back into the carriage and don't even think of doing anything stupid."

The voice behind the gun was male, firm and sounded well educated, at least from his accent, by virtue of being pretty much devoid of one. Billy decided that for the moment he should do as he was told. Turning to his right, with the gunman still at his back, Billy faced the carriage. He looked down the length of it and saw the boy he had watched chain his bicycle to the pole. He was also holding a gun. It was also pointed at Billy. Glancing over his shoulder, Billy saw that the two hijackers were similarly dressed. They wore trousers, over which hung loose shirts, with printed black and white ethnic scarves around their neck. Both had sandals on their feet, which were bare. The boy at the end of the carriage had a straggly beard and shaven head.

"Sit down and don't speak."

Again Billy did as he was told, lowering himself into the first available seat. He was then able to turn and look up at his captor. Although the hijacker's features were those of a young man, he had dark malignant pools for eyes. Billy levelly met his gaze and in it saw something more than the thrill of the situation the man was now in charge of. It was the age old look of fervour. His eyes reflected things he had seen that he shouldn't have, coupled with the look of one that has total belief in his cause. Whatever that cause might be. A cause Billy would hear about in due course.

"Give me your phone," the man demanded.

"I don't have one," Billy said.

"Don't play games with me. I can see the earpiece. Now do as you're told and give it to me."

"It's an iPod, not a phone. I lost my phone so I don't have one. Here," said Billy and thrust the iPod at the man who was trying to intimidate him into submission. But Sgt Billy Williams wasn't easily intimidated and had never been known to submit to anyone. Well, anyone apart from Sgt Major Crane that was. And maybe his Officer Commanding, Captain Draper, or even the CO of his Military Police Regiment. Yes, he'd submit to anyone of those three men. But certainly not to the piece of shit pointing a gun at him. For now he would co-operate, but that was all.

Looking at the iPod as if was something extremely distasteful, the man threw it on the floor and stamped on it. "There," he said with a toss of his head that made his black curls shake underneath the bandanna that was holding it out of his eyes. "Whatever it is, you can't use it anymore."

Turning to the other passengers in the carriage he said, "I want your phones, laptops and tablets." As the passengers looked at him in stunned silence, he shouted, "Now, not next week. Now!"

That galvanised them and each started to pat pockets, check bags and unplug earphones. Whilst his fellow passengers were fumbling for their devices, Billy took the opportunity to study the other captives. For that was what they were now, Billy surmised. Captives, who were at the mercy of several young men and their demands.

Billy was sitting in a row of two high backed seats, with a table separating him from the two seats opposite. Next to him, by the window, was an older man, dressed in a business suit, made from shiny grey material. He was sweating profusely and dabbing his face with a handkerchief that he had pulled from the top pocket of his jacket. Waves of the man's fear washed over Billy.

Opposite them were two women. One was heavily pregnant, wearing dark leggings coupled with a voluminous shirt. Her long straight mousey hair was scraped back from her face. Any flush of well-being she may have had from her biological state had gone. She looked at Billy with eyes that implored him to help her. But, of course, for the moment he was as helpless as she was.

The other woman was younger, wearing large dark rimmed glasses, making her look intellectual and bookish. Her dark hair had strands of red in which glinted in the shaft of sunlight falling on her from the large carriage window. She was looking around, more with interest than fear and as her eyes lit upon Billy she gave him a small conspiratorial smile. He decided that of the three people surrounding him, she would be the most useful. Should he have the opportunity of overpowering one or more of their captors in the future.

As far as he could remember, there were just the four of them in this carriage, but he wasn't sure how many there were in the other one. He did know for certain that the train comprised of just two carriages. As they'd stopped at the small stations since leaving Carlisle, many passengers had hopped on and off the train. Some of them tourists, marked as such by their walking boots and rucksacks and some locals juggling shopping bags, umbrellas and coats. The conductor was definitely in the other carriage, but that was all Billy was sure of. There was no point in trying to figure it out, so he decided to concentrate on his own situation.

Focusing on the hijackers, he saw there were now four men, as two others had just joined them from the neighbouring carriage. Secure in the knowledge that their colleagues had the passengers under control by virtue of guns trained on them, the two walked down the aisle, pulling rolls of dark paper out of their rucksacks. Moving up and down the carriage, they roughly pushed and pulled the hostages out of the way, whilst they placed the paper over the windows and secured it with thick, strong, tape. Immediately the carriage was plunged into an eyrie half light. The gloom serving to focus the hostages' minds on their situation. Leaving them and Billy, in no doubt that this was a serious hijack. And that for the moment, the young men were in complete control of the situation.

Once the paper was in place covering all the windows, two of the men turned towards the door leading to the driver's cab. A shot rang out, causing screams from some of the passengers, as the hijackers blasted out the lock. Billy leaned out into the aisle to see two men disappear into the driver's cab. He was unable to see anything else, as he was immediately ordered to sit back in his seat. A further two hijackers pushed and shoved three more passengers from the second carriage, into the set of four seats across the aisle from Billy.

Having deposited their human cargo, they then returned to the second carriage. As they slammed the door behind them, the train driver was bundled through the cab door and roughly pushed into a vacant seat. At the sight of the driver, a feeling of resignation seemed to come over the hostages, who deflated like balloons. The realisation hitting them that without a driver, the train was going nowhere. They were trapped. Billy watched any fight they may have had in them drain away, as shoulders slumped and eyes dulled.

Billy now knew there were eight passengers, all in the same carriage. Two terrorists were in the second carriage, no doubt look-outs. There were two with guns trained on them in this carriage and then a further two hijackers who had stayed in the driver's cab. Billy needed to get this information to Crane. He needed to let him know there were six terrorists and eight hostages. But how soon would he be allowed to use the facilities so he could retrieve his mobile? And when he was, would he be allowed any privacy?

11:00 hours

"This is the BBC News at One," the sonorous voice of the radio presenter filled Sgt Major Crane's car as he raced northward along the motorway. "A group of hijackers have taken control of a train travelling on the Carlisle to Settle railway. Initial reports suggest the two carriage train has stopped in the middle of the Ribble viaduct. The following statement has been received by the News Agency Reuters and simultaneously reported on various human rights websites:

Recently, 65 prisoners were released from Bagram Detention Centre by President Hamid Karzia.

This was a bold move by the President of Afghanistan, aimed at correcting the wrongs done to the Afghan people by the US and UK administrations. However, the release of 65 prisoners was not enough. Not nearly enough.

We therefore want the government of the United Kingdom to release further prisoners. Those innocent men and women illegally detained indefinitely by the British military forces. We will issue a list of the detainees to be released in due course.

In the meantime, we are holding the passengers of this train hostage. They are being held illegally and against their will. Innocent people who have nothing to do with the struggle against the Taliban in Afghanistan. Just like the guiltless prisoners entombed in Bagram.

The remainder of the news bulletin was drowned out by Crane's expletives. It hadn't taken more than a few minutes for him to react to Billy's earlier phone call to him at Provost Barracks. Grabbing his mobile phone off his desk, he'd run up the stairs and burst into Captain Draper's office. Foregoing the usual, required, formalities and sliding to a halt in front of Draper's desk, he'd succinctly relayed Billy's predicament. Draper readily agreed to alert the security forces and approved Crane's current dash up the motorway, pushing him out of the office with one hand, whilst reaching for his phone with the other.

Crane didn't know what would greet him upon his arrival at Ribblehead, but logic presumed there would now be a few hours of 'settling in'. The hijackers had made their demands and would now be concentrating on keeping the train and the hostages secure. The police, security services and army would be getting their people in place and appointing a negotiator. The television stations and reporters would be doing something similar. Getting their outside broadcast vans as close to the incident as possible and pulling reporters off other stories to cover the biggest news item in Britain since the 7/7 bombings. No doubt some news programme anchors would be sent to Ribblehead. What could have greater impact, than to present the whole evening news programme with the train marooned on the track as the backdrop?

Crane wondered how Billy was faring, his young, easy going, happy-go-lucky Special Investigations Branch sergeant. In his mind he saw Billy's engaging smile, eyes as blue as a Mediterranean sky and blond hair kept as long as regulations allowed. A tall striking figure - but not immediately recognisable as military. Crane hoped that would work in Billy's favour, for if the hijackers were to discover his military background, it could compromise not only his safety but the safety of his fellow hostages. The last thing Billy needed was for the hostage-takers to realise they had one of the hated British Army in their midst. That thought made Crane increase the pressure of his foot on the accelerator pedal. His hands squeezed the steering wheel as though he were squeezing the life out of one of the captors, by strangling him with his bare hands.

11:15 hours

Someone else steaming up the motorway in a northerly direction was Diane Chambers, self styled investigative reporter for the Aldershot News. A provincial paper, part of a group of newspapers covering the county of Hampshire. Her young legs, clad in jeans, were trembling with excitement as she listened to the same news bulletin as Crane. She'd seen Crane a few minutes earlier, sat in his car, waiting in a line of traffic to get onto the motorway. Tension had radiated from him. Hands gripping the steering wheel, he'd gunned his engine and swung his head from side to side, as he'd impatiently waited for a gap in the traffic.

Her radar was always on high alert whenever she saw Crane in that sort of mood. He'd provided her with yards of copy in the past, from murders and bombs, to an expose of military secrets. So putting two and two together and making five, Diane decided there must be a connection between Crane and the hijacked train. Which meant a connection to Aldershot.

Ignoring the protests from her editor, that were spewing out of her hands-free mobile phone, she had swung her car around and followed Crane onto the motorway. To start with she was working blind. Had no idea where he was going, but convinced that wherever it was, she needed to be going there as well. And now she knew, thanks to the BBC news broadcast. She was as focused on her mission as no doubt Crane was, without any thought of how long it would take her to get to Yorkshire or the fact that she had no change of clothes with her. She had her coat, computer, small digital recorder and her purse, which was all an impulsive, ambitious reporter needed.

Cutting across her editor's remonstrations she shouted, "Look, Crane wouldn't take off like that without a very good reason. Which must mean a local connection between Aldershot and this train hijack. If you don't want me to go, then I'm officially on leave. I've got a couple of weeks owing." The response to that was silence, so Diane continued, "But if I'm right, then I'm on the clock. Fair enough?"

As her editor gruffly conceded, she decided to push her luck. "In the meantime, get someone to do some background on the Ribblehead Viaduct. I'm going to need it for the piece you're going to splash all over the front page of next week's paper."

She ended the call, cutting off his laughter. He wouldn't be laughing soon, she thought. He'd be falling all over her for copy. Just as soon as she found the connection, that was. To make the miles go quicker she ran over her knowledge of Crane. A tough, no nonsense investigator, he'd proverbially pulled the wool over her eyes on more than one occasion. Yet he wasn't beyond using her services when it suited him. He was married with one son, but she didn't think it would be his family that were on the train. Although he was from the Newcastle area, his wife Tina was a southerner born and bred, so Diane doubted Tina would be in Yorkshire. That left Crane's crew. It must be someone close to him, she figured. An anonymous soldier would be a worry, but that worry would belong to the military no doubt already gathering at Ribblehead. It wouldn't be personal to Crane.

As her mobile was on hands free, she risked looking at it and dialled a number. It was quickly answered by a woman.

"Good morning, is it possible to speak to the Padre, please?" Diane asked her.

"Certainly," the female voice replied, "I'll just get him for you."

Chambers cut the line, not needing to speak to the Padre, or his wife Kim. She now knew the connection wasn't Kim, Crane's ex-office manager, nor Captain Symmonds, Padre of the Garrison Church, both close to Crane and accomplices in previous investigations.

Diane had one more call to make, to Provost Barracks. Asking to speak to Captain Draper, she was told he was in a meeting. But her next request hit the jackpot.

"Can I speak to Sgt Billy Williams then please?" she said.

"Sorry, miss, he's on leave at the moment."

"Lucky sod," Diane retorted. "I wish I was on a sunny beach somewhere."

The soldier laughed. "No such luck there. Sgt Williams is visiting his parents in Carlisle. Can I take a message?"

"No, no message. Thank you."

Diane cut the call. She'd found the connection. Billy must be on the train. But she didn't feel exuberant about that piece of information. Not at all. She obviously knew Billy in a professional capacity. But they'd bumped into each other socially a few times and had a laugh and a few drinks together. But on Friday they were due to meet by arrangement. A date. The thought had previously made her smile. Now it scared her. Would he still be alive by Friday, she wondered, as sweat trickled down her face and slicked her hands on the steering wheel.

12:00 hours

Billy was squirming, trying to get comfortable on the train seat that he'd no doubt have to get used to, even though there wasn't enough room for his lanky legs. He thought about the last time he'd been on a train. Just two days earlier, when he was returning home, going to visit his parents who lived in Carlisle. Going back to see his mum for a couple of days, to eat her Sunday lunch, leave some money on the mantelpiece so she could treat herself, give her a hug and a kiss until next time. Or at least that had been the plan.

Not that Billy minded visiting her, he loved his mum to bits, of course he did. It was just that he didn't like being away from the lads. He was proud of his military service and his regiment and preferred to be close to the body of men that were his real home and family these days, no matter where in Britain, or abroad, they were posted.

Last weekend his idea had been that after the hellos and welcomes, he'd go with his old man to the local boozer and sink a few pints, which were essential to helping Billy sleep in the small lumpy bed he'd had since he was a child. He always enjoyed his few snatched hours with his father and his cronies whenever he could find the time to visit. The local Working Men's Club reminded him of the camaraderie of the Sergeant's Mess. The club was pitched right in the middle of the Mount Pleasant Housing Estate in Carlisle. Unfortunately there was nothing pleasant about the estate. A jumble of people, cars, discarded appliances and dogs summed up most of the area. A real live 'Benefit Street'. His mum and dad lived on the fringe of the estate, in a quieter part, mostly inhabited by elderly residents.

On his walk from the train to his parent's house last Friday, he'd met May, a relative from his large extended family. A younger sibling on his mum's side, although there wasn't anything young about May anymore. The older generation of the Williams family still lived clustered together around a couple of streets on Mount Pleasant Estate. The younger generation having left years ago, mostly going to the South of England to find work.

But instead of just sharing a cup of coffee and enjoying each other's company, May was jumpy and upset. He'd finally got her to confess that the behaviour of one of local gangs was getting out of hand. They were stealing cars and mugging people for a few quid and their mobile phones. Breaking into empty houses and then selling the stolen stuff to riffraff from other estates. The residents thought maybe the youths needed to steal to fuel their drug habits. Either that or it was done out of boredom. They weren't really sure. But whatever the reason, it was frightening the life out of the older residents. Billy was upset enough to find that they were harassing May, but positively angry that the behaviour was also affecting his Mum and Dad. He'd promised May that he'd sort it out, but without revealing who he was. Telling her he'd be the soul of discretion.

Dragging his thoughts back to the present, Billy acknowledged that now he had another problem to sort out. But a much more deadly one than a gang of youths roaming the local streets. Here was also a gang of youths, but this time they were in charge of a train, not a few streets on a housing estate. Young men armed with automatic weapons and hand guns, instead of unarmed kids. Altogether a much more deadly and dangerous proposition.

14:00 hours

The young police constable at the barrier set up in front of Ribblehead railway station, eyed Crane nervously. "I'm not allowed to let just anyone pass, sir," he said, his large Adam's apple bobbing up and down in his throat as he spoke. "And you're not on my list," he said and rather needlessly held up his clipboard.

"I totally understand that," said Crane smoothly, trying not to get distracted by the young man's unfortunate physical appendage. "But, you see, I'm not just anyone. I'm Sgt Major Crane of the Special Investigations Branch of the Royal Military Police," and Crane lifted the identification worn around his neck and poked it in the young man's face. "I must have access to the control centre. I've inside information about the hijacked train that I guarantee they'll want to hear."

Captain Draper had earlier supplied the information about the location of the men who were to be the 'boots on the ground' as it were. Those nearest to the hijacked train and who would make the tactical decisions. However, Draper had been unable to gain Crane official access, making Crane rely on his wits to get around the cordons.

"Well, um, well, I'm not sure, sir."

The young man looked around, probably hoping someone would come and save him. Crane, however, was hoping they wouldn't.

"Well, don't you worry, because I am sure. In the station building are they?" Crane asked and as the police constable turned to look where he was indicating, Crane ducked under the hastily erected tape and sprinted for the Victorian structure. The station entrance was guarded by a soldier and Crane knew that all he had to do was to get to him, to ensure access.

With, "Oy, come back here," being shouted at his back, Crane ran on, black suit jacket flapping and regimental tie askew. He slowed as he approached the soldier guarding the station building, who had been watching the altercation. However, instead of challenging Crane, he stood to attention. Crane's dark suit and regimental tie over his crisp white shirt - his normal SIB civilian uniform - and with his identification around his neck, ensured instant recognition from the soldier on duty.

"Sir." The soldier acknowledged Crane's presence but did not salute, even though Crane was of superior rank. Being out of army uniform meant that a salute from the lesser ranking man wasn't required. The soldier signalled to the young police constable, with a nod of his head, that Crane's presence was in order.

"Afternoon," Crane replied. "I understand that this is the command centre for the hijacked train."

"That's correct, sir."

"Then I need to be inside."

"That's not possible, sir. My orders are that no one can disturb the meeting."

Crane said. "Would you let me in if I told you there

was a sergeant from the Royal Military Police on the train? And that he is communicating with me via mobile phone? I believe that makes me a vital part of the investigation."

The beauty of the Branch was that its investigators cut across the military rank system when on an active case and as far as Crane was concerned Billy being on the hijacked train made it an active investigation.

The soldier blanched at the news and sharply stepped aside. "Very well, sir," he said and allowed Crane access to the station building. Crane nodded his thanks, opened the door and stepped into the large waiting room. In the open space, three men stood around a trestle table on which a large scale ordnance survey map was taped. Two of them were in army uniform and one in civilian clothing. They were all looking at the map as if it held the answer to their unspoken question - what the hell do we do next? No one seemed to have noticed that Crane had slipped in and quietly closed the door behind him. He stood against the high stone wall, which gave off a slight chill and settled down to observe.

"Obviously the first priority is to ensure the safety of the hostages," the civilian said, his voice bouncing off the high ceiling. He was a small dapper man, his suit as well cut as his hair.

"I realise that, but the army's first priority is to get them out of there."

Crane didn't recognise the speaker but his uniform identified him as holding the rank of Colonel.

"We can't just dive in, for God's sake," the diminutive civilian replied and started pacing the room, his words quickening with his steps. "We've got to at least try and talk to the hijackers. Start a dialogue.

Persuade them to let the hostages go. Launching an immediate, brutal attack without previously exhausting the potential for a negotiated solution, might inflame the extremist's cause still further." He stopped, turned towards the Colonel and implored, "And God knows what the British public would think."

"Caring what the British public think is your job, not mine. Nor am I going to pander to your bosses in Whitehall and Westminster. My only concern is as principal operational advisor to my senior officers. I'm the one who says when, if, and how we go in. So, if we knew something about these bloody hijackers, it might help. Have we got any background on them yet?" the Colonel snapped in exasperation as he looked across the table to a young soldier that Crane recognised.

Corporal Dudley-Jones was in the Intelligence Service and had assisted Crane when they worked together on a security case. Their task had been to keep the athletes of Team GB safe whilst they were on Aldershot Garrison in the run-up to the 2012 Olympic Games.

"At the moment, sir," Dudley-Jones said, "we don't think they're part of a recognised faction, but army and civilian intelligence services are doing their best to get us as much information as they can on who might be involved in such an operation. We're also working with the NCA, to see what they have on their books that might help. That's the newly formed National Crime Agency, sir," he explained to the Colonel's blank expression.

"And how the bloody hell do you intend to find out who's holding the train and passengers to ransom?" the Colonel shouted.

"Oh, Dudley-Jones here will be listening to the

'chatter' on the airways and on the internet, I expect. Not to mention running facial recognition software. If the group can be found on any CCTV footage, that is. In fact any intelligence, IT and communications will all be analysed and used to help us deal with these bloody idiots," Crane said, coming to Dudley-Jones' rescue. It seemed the lad hadn't lost his rather embarrassing habit of his face suffusing with colour when he was put under pressure and not sure how to reply to a question. He was a very intelligent young soldier, but one who was happier communicating with his computer, rather than face to face with human beings.

Whirling around, the Colonel snarled at Crane, "Who the bloody hell are you and how did you get in here?"

"Sgt Major Crane, SIB." Crane deliberately left the 'sir' part out of his answer, in response to the man's obnoxious attitude.

"We don't need help from the SIB, Crane, so you can go back to wherever the hell it is you came from."

"I wouldn't be that hasty if I were you, sir, as I have information that can help." Crane bristled at the Colonel's attitude but tried hard to keep his contempt for the man under control, at least until he was safely established as a necessary part of the command team.

"Do enlighten us, Sgt Major," the civilian asked with a sharp sliver of sarcasm in his voice. "Do share your knowledge."

"How many hijackers and hostages are on the train?" Crane replied by asking a question of his own, deliberately leaning nonchalantly against the door and looking around with a slight smile on his face.

"At the moment, we don't know, sir," Dudley-Jones answered, Crane's ally in a room full of hissing snakes.

So Crane told them. "There are 6 hijackers and minimum of 4 hostages."

"How the bloody hell do you know that? Have the SIB added clairvoyance to their list of attributes?" Clearly the Colonel had a very low opinion of the Branch and Crane was very much looking forward to putting him in his place.

"Because - " But before Crane could continue, his phone beeped with a message. Pulling it out of his pocket and reading it, Crane then looked up and grinned at the assembled men. "Sorry, make that 8 hostages and 6 hijackers." Looking around at the silent, gaping faces he said, "My sergeant, Billy Williams, is on the train and has managed to keep his mobile hidden from the hijackers. So I think that makes me a vital member of your team, don't you?"

15:00 hours

Diane Chambers had also made it to Yorkshire. But without Crane's credentials, she was penned in with the press. They were mostly acting like chickens, occasionally pecking at the floor as they looked at and checked their equipment and then raising their heads to look around, eyes darting from one side to the other, desperate not to miss any slight movement from the train and therefore missing the shot. The one that would be beamed around the world.

From their vantage point, the Ribble Viaduct looked both an imposing structure and at the same time smaller than she had imagined. The further back from it you were, the harder it was to see the scale of the massive stone arches. The only point of reference was the train. A blue, white and purple, two carriage train, looking as small and insignificant as a toy, perched on top of the middle arches.

Unusually for Diane, who was aiming to be a hardened investigative news reporter, her thoughts turned to the passengers marooned on the train. She could only speculate how they were feeling. Frightened? Cowed? Upset? Rather them than her, she thought, not sure she would have the stomach for dealing with enforced incarceration.

She had collected a press pack on her arrival, but it contained scant information. For the moment there was no news from the authorities as to how many passengers were on the train. It wasn't known if they were male or female, young or old, nor whom they might be. An emergency contact number had been issued, asking for people who thought a relative could be on the train to ring the authorities, in order to try and answer those questions. Unfortunately, unlike air travel, trains did not have passenger manifests, especially local trains such as this one, where most tickets were bought from a ticket machine. Nor did the authorities, at the moment, know how many hijackers there were. So the press were left awaiting a press briefing, promised to be held in an hour's time.

Try as she might to stop them, her thoughts kept turning to Billy. They'd met accidentally one evening in the Goose pub in Aldershot, when both were at a loose end, and had decided to abate hostilities and have a drink together. Promising not to talk about work had broken the ice and one drink had turned into several, accompanied by much fun and laughter. The evening had ended by Billy taking her personal mobile number and leaving her with a kiss on her cheek. As she thought about that evening and their pre-arranged date for this coming Friday, her face burned. Forcing herself to put her personal feelings to one side, she focused on her job. But couldn't help the lingering thought - I hope to God he's alright.

16:00 hours

All the passengers were now in one carriage and had managed to introduce themselves to each other. Billy looked around at the motley crew and wondered who would be brave enough to help him should he be able to distract the hijackers and possibly take one or more of them out. The train driver, Mick, was making a good show of hiding his fear. He was a small, rotund man, who's belly hung over the belt of his trousers. The middle-aged conductor, Peggy, was comforting the pregnant woman who was called Hazel and glaring at the nearest hijacker. The hijackers had relieved her of her ticket machine, which now lay discarded in a corner of the carriage. The bulky sweating man was Colin and the bookish looking girl was called Emma. A further two passengers had joined them from the other carriage, a man and his son in walking gear. The father, David, was doing a fair job of reassuring his son Charlie, who Billy thought was probably 11 or 12 years old. The boy seemed to swing between fascination at the situation he and his father found themselves in, interspersed with bouts of crying. Allowing his underlying emotions to come to the fore. Indicating that really he was only a child, despite all his bravado.

Billy had managed to get a further message to Crane by asking the young men holding them hostage to allow the passengers to take a toilet break. But he knew he wouldn't have another chance to send a text for a few hours. He wouldn't be able to pull that stunt again too soon, without the hijackers becoming suspicious. So far no one had offered a reason for them being held captive, so Billy decided to try and find out.

Turning casually to the young man standing beside him, who was leaning against the side of the seats with his gun trained on the hostages, Billy said, "I think it's about time you told us what's going on and who the hell you all are."

He hadn't meant for his last few words to come out as aggressively as they had, but they prompted demands from the other passengers as well.

"Yeah, it's about time you lot told us why we're here," that was from Mick the driver. "There's going to be trouble from the railway over this, you know," he continued. "Have you any idea how disruptive this is going to be to the rail network? Hundreds of passenger trains and freight trains run on this route." Mick shook his bald head in disbelief. "It's going to be a bloody nightmare," he finished.

"We don't much care about the disruption," came the reply. "In fact the more disruption the better. But you both have a point. It is about time you understood that you are being held against your will, until the authorities decide to liberate our brothers being wrongly held in Bagram Detention Centre."

"What?" Mick said. "What the bloody hell do we have to do with people in this Bagram Detention Centre. I don't even know where the hell that is!"

"Afghanistan, old man. It's in Afghanistan. Tell me, do you have any brothers?"

"Brothers?" Mick's confusion was evident from his puckered brow, but he replied, "Alright, I've got a brother, what about it?"

"And is your brother free to go about his business, his daily life, without fear of being pulled off the streets and thrown in jail on a made-up charge?"

"Of course he is."

"Well, my brother isn't. Our demands are simple. We want the UK authorities to release members of our families being held against their will in Bagram and when they do, we'll release you."

As that information sunk in, there were varied reactions. Emma said, "How long is that going to take?" She pushed her glasses up off her face onto the top of her head, so they nestled in her hair.

"What's your name?" the hijacker demanded.

"Emma," she replied. "What's yours? If you are doing this to us, we have a right to know who we're dealing with."

"Our names are irrelevant. All that matters is that we have guns trained on you and as long as you and the authorities co-operate, then no one's going to get hurt."

"Now look here," Colin said, the sheen of sweat making his head shine, reminding Billy of a bowling ball. "This is an outrage. I've got a company to run and meetings to go to. I can't just sit here, you've got to let us go," he gabbled and began to rise from his seat.

"Sit down!"

But the large man ignored the instruction and stood up.

"I said sit down!" The hijacker's words were accompanied by a backward swing of his arm, ready to smash the butt of his gun into Colin's head.

As he brought down his arm in an arc towards Colin, Billy rose to try and protect his fellow captor.

That was when the phone in the driver's cab started to ring.

16:00 hours

The police hostage negotiator brought in by the Major Incident Squad was nothing like Crane imagined. In American films they were usually tough, no nonsense, little talking and flawed human beings. The flawed bit being important for the narrative of the film. But Mike Keane was none of those things. At least on first appearances. He was tall and slim with sandy brown hair, but what impressed Crane was his calmness, his stillness. Keane listened to the briefing with little reaction and absolutely no fidgeting. He asked probing questions every now and again, especially of Crane about Billy's involvement, and from Dudley-Jones about the information, or rather lack of it, that they had on the terrorists so far. But other than that he remained still and silent. Occasionally he made notes in the legal-type blue A4 notebook he'd brought with him.

At the end of the briefing he said, "Thank you gentlemen for your succinct assessment of the situation."

Very polite, Crane thought.

"Can you direct me to the phone that's been connected to the train?"

Crane nodded in the direction of the shop, which was part of the visitor's centre and situated behind a door off the main waiting area. The team had taken over the whole of Ribblehead Station to use as their headquarters. Refurbished over 10 years ago, the station was quite large. There were exhibition rooms dedicated to the building of the Carlisle to Settle railway and a shop on the ground floor. Up above was a caretaker's flat and just down the track the Station Master's House. Both sets of accommodation had been taken over and the whole team were staying in-situ. Crane doubted they'd get much sleep, but at least it meant it was possible to have a bit of down time and a shower.

"It's in the shop, said Crane. "We've had the shop items cleared to give you more room and Northern Rail have linked the phone directly into the driver's cab on the train. No other calls can be made from or to that handset, so you'll have unrestricted access to the train. Always assuming they answer the phone, that is."

Keane nodded and went to go through the door.

"Keane!" Crane's shout stopped him. "Don't drop my Sergeant in it. If you do, I won't be responsible for my actions."

Keane simply turned and smiled. "Don't worry, Sgt Major, I'm well aware of any repercussions should I make a mistake like that," he said. "Please rest assured I have no intention of 'dropping him in it' as you so colourfully put it. I've done this job before. So if you'll excuse me, I want to try and make the first contact. Then we can see where we go from there."

Crane wasn't sure whether to be reassured or incensed by the man's calm exterior. He could only hope Keane could remain as calm as he was now, under the kind of pressure he was likely to face over the coming hours or even days. He turned away as Keane went through to the shop.

"What's Keane's background?" asked the civil servant that Crane now knew to be Andrew Hardwick. He was from one or other of the intelligence services, MI5 or MI6 or some such. Or even from a service that had no name and no-one knew about. Amongst Hardwick's many roles was to keep the Prime Minister and his COBRA team updated on events as they unfolded.

"He's a psychologist, apparently," the Colonel said.

"A practicing one? A clinical psychologist who's called on by the police?"

"No, he's a policeman. He graduated as a psychologist but because of his interest in the criminal mind, instead of becoming an independent forensic psychologist, he decided to join the force on the fast track graduate program, wanting to combine his knowledge of psychology with police work. So now he's an expert that can be called on whenever there's a situation like this."

Crane said, "Surely there aren't many situations like this?"

"You'd be surprised, Crane," Hardwick replied. "Not everything is reported in the press, you know."

"Well I hope he knows his bloody job," Crane snapped and turned towards Dudley-Jones, who was at his laptop, ready to amplify the call through speakers he had recently attached to it.

Everyone fell silent and turned towards the laptop, as the sound of a ringing telephone filled the waiting room.

16:10 hours

Kourash knew the call would come. Knew they'd try and contact him and try to talk him into giving himself up. Even though he was half expecting it, the ringing telephone had surprised him and everyone else. Kourash slowly dropped the arm he had raised in anger. Perhaps now wasn't the time to upset the hostages, he decided. It would only make any brave ones amongst them determined to try and get themselves out of this situation. Not that he thought anyone one of them capable of such an act. And anyway, being marooned in a train, 100 ft above the ground in the middle of a viaduct didn't make for an easy get away. Should one of them be foolish enough to try, there were guards posted at both ends of the train, ready to gun them down.

The telephone continued its incessant ringing as Kourash moved towards the driver's cab. He motioned for the two guards stationed there to leave the confined space and once he had closed the door behind them, he picked up the phone.

And didn't speak.

He could hear a man breathing on the other end of the line. Kourash was determined not to be the one to break the silence, so he sat in the driver's seat, phone to his ear, and raised the blind that had been pulled down to cover the window from prying eyes. He looked out across the pleasing vista of the Yorkshire Dales. It was a tranquil, yet typically British, view. The sun came and went as large clusters of clouds raced across the sky. Sheep grazed on the nearby hills. Clusters of rocks dotted the area, their granite sparkling in the sunshine. He was, of course, looking at the view facing away from the inward curves of the viaduct, looking in the opposite direction to where the might of the British Government was no doubt plotting the best way to get him to let the hostages go. And the man on the other end of the telephone was their first offensive strike.

"Hello, I'm Mike."

Kourash had done it. Scored the first point. Made the man speak first.

"What's your name?" Mike asked.

After a long pause, he eventually replied, "Kourash."

"Well, Kourash, I'm here to listen to your..."

Kourash placed the receiver back on the telephone, cutting Mike off. That would do for now. He had scored the first point. He closed his eyes and whispered, "I'll get justice for you, Feda. Your incarceration will not have been in vain. I promise I'll get you released."

Mike Keane walked back into the briefing room to face the four men who had turned towards him. All had an opinion they wanted to voice. Well three of them did. Crane knew that Dudley-Jones was of a far too lowly a rank, to have an opinion.

"Well, that didn't go well," Colonel Booth was the first to criticise. "Not much dialogue there."

"I thought it went extremely well," Keane replied

evenly. Crane thought that if Keane was a successful hostage negotiator, then dealing with this small band of experts would no doubt be a picnic compared to some situations he'd been in. Colonel Booth wasn't likely to ruffle Keane, he'd more than likely come up against worse.

"How come?" Crane asked, echoing Keane's even tone. The man had something there, Crane thought. Perhaps he should try and cultivate an even tone and an unruffled exterior, for future use. But no. It didn't take Crane long to decide that he was a 'hard as nails' investigator. It wouldn't do for him to go soft, or at least appear to have gone soft.

"I got his name," Keane replied to Crane's question.

"And?"

"And so I scored the first point. I got him to tell me something, without giving anything away."

"Is that the way you think he'll see it?" Hardwick wanted to know.

After a pause, Keane replied, "I expect he'll think he's got one over on me, because he made me speak first. But that's fine."

"Why is that fine?" Crane asked, becoming genuinely interested in the psychological approach.

"Because the more Kourash thinks he has the upper hand, the more confident he'll become. Meaning that he's more likely to miss something in the future. In the meantime, I'd like Dudley-Jones to see what he can do with the name Kourash."

"I'm already on it, sir," said Dudley-Jones, peering at his computer screen. "His name means 'ancient king'. Maybe that's why he thinks he's a leader of men, thinks he's their king. Kings often think they're indestructible. His parent's must have thought he was something special to choose that name for him. If he's been brought up with that attitude then..."

"Precisely," said Keane, "good job, Dudley-Jones."

The young man once again made his embarrassment evident.

"Mumbo, jumbo, rubbish," was Crane's opinion. He'd had enough of the soft approach bollocks already and growled, "What's in a name, for God's sake?"

"Far more than you would think," replied Keane. "Especially when we're talking about people from different ethnic origins to our own. In Kourash's culture, names are chosen far more for their meaning than here in England, where they're chosen for their popularity. Think how many George's there are going to be now - just because the latest member of the Royal Family is called George."

"Still think it's a load of rubbish," mumbled Crane, whose own name was Tom, shortened from Thomas, meaning the doubter.

17:00 hours

Harry Poole, senior reporter on the Daily Record newspaper, had made his way up from London to Yorkshire and after several hours of driving, had finally made it to the first police check point. He'd actually wanted to travel up to Yorkshire by train, which would have given him more time to do research on the viaduct and the rail system during the journey. But because of the cancellations and delays caused to the network by the train siege, it hadn't been possible.

After showing his press pass to the policeman on duty, he was directed to a large car park from where he could walk to the press coral. And that's precisely what it was. The press were herded into a cordoned-off field, where various television crews and local and national reporters had set up shop. Harry turned at the noise of a lorry behind him and watched as mobile toilets were brought into the field, followed by a couple of outside catering vans. No doubt the smell of burgers and sausages would soon mingle with the smell of fascination and excitement emanating from the press. He was reminded of packs of hungry wolves, as the television crews and presenters vied for the best spot for their live reports. It seemed everyone wanted to have the viaduct as their backdrop and heated arguments were breaking out between rival stations. Harry knew it would only be a matter of time before crews from other countries arrived as well, particularly if it looked like the siege was going to drag on for some days, as indicated by the provision of mobile facilities.

As he threaded his way through the crowd, searching for friendly faces, he glimpsed a familiar checked shirt and jeans, topped by black curly hair. It couldn't be, could it, he thought? Surely Diane Chambers hadn't arrived so quickly? What did she know that he didn't?

Approaching her from behind, he was able to listen to her strident, hissed telephone call.

"Look, I really do need to speak to Sgt Major Crane, I know he's here. I also know why he's here."

She didn't listen to the person on the other end of the line for long before saying, "Oh very well, tell him I know about Billy and if he doesn't ring me soon, I'll print it. Tell him he's got an hour."

Harry stood rooted to the spot, stunned, as he watched Diane walk away. He couldn't get his head around it. Billy was on the train? Jesus Christ. But more to the point, would Crane get the message? Harry knew Diane couldn't be allowed to print that sort of information. But what could he do to stop her?

He ambled over to a quieter part of the field, mulling over his problem. Coming to a decision he pulled his phone out of his pocket and rang a number that had been stored in his phone directory for the past couple of years, but rarely used.

Crane looked at the piece of paper that had just been handed to him and read the words written there with increasing anger. Crushing the paper in his hand, he pulled out his mobile phone. But instead of using it, he turned it over several times, weighing up his options and deciding he had very few of them. It was a conundrum that definitely called for a cigarette.

He was just lighting one, after ambling outside, when his phone buzzed. Hoping it might be Billy he dropped his cigarette in his haste to answer his mobile.

A voice said, "Crane, it's me. Looks like you've got a problem with Diane Chambers."

"Tell me about it, Harry," replied Crane, disappointed the call wasn't from Billy, but on the other hand relieved. Harry could be just the solution he'd been searching for. He bent down to collect his cigarette and his thoughts. "Wait a minute, where are you?" he said as he straightened up. "How do you know about Diane Chambers?"

"I'm in the press field, about half a mile away from you, if my guess is right."

"Right on the button, as usual, Harry."

"That's what I thought when I heard her leaving a message for you. Is it true? Is Billy on the train? If he is, we can't let her print it."

"Don't I know it. I was just trying to figure out what to do when you phoned. And there you were, like manna from Heaven."

"Alright, you old bugger, what do you want me to do?"

Crane said, "Well, we all know Diane Chambers has delusions of grandeur, right?"

"Right." Poole elongated the word, as if doubting he wanted to hear Crane's solution.

"So, how about if we offer her a job with you?"

"Jesus Christ, Crane. You can't be serious."

"Deadly serious, Harry. Think about it. You're going to need help." Crane walked along the platform as he spoke. "Someone to gather background for you on the railway, terrorists and Bagram Detention Centre, liaise with other members of the press pack, organise photos etc. And I'm sure the on-line version of your paper will need keeping up to date with events as they happen. So if Chambers was to help with that sort of stuff, it would leave you free to write the big pieces. And it would make her feel important, give her an opportunity to work with a national paper, play to her ambitions."

"And in return?"

"And in return she keeps her mouth shut about Billy being on that train. We can't let that leak and risk the hijackers finding out about him. At the moment he's the only conduit we have giving us information."

"Bloody hell, he's been in touch?"

"Yes and you can have all the gory details afterwards for an exclusive if you help me out. We have to keep him safe. I'm sure she'll understand if it's explained properly."

"Ah, the old carrot and stick routine."

"Precisely."

"But this time, I'm the bloody carrot."

"Well, I suppose you could put it that way," Crane smiled for the first time that day. "Please, Harry," he said, suddenly serious again.

It only took Harry a moment to agree to Crane's request. After all Crane had given him good copy from previous investigations, so it was only fair to help him out. "Go on then, I'll do it. But you owe me one for this, Crane."

18:45 hours

Night was falling and with the fading light, so hope faded for the hostages trapped in the train. It was as if the reality of their situation had finally hit them, every passing hour pummelling them with thoughts of home.

It was hard to tell who was faring worst, Charlie the young boy or Colin the bulky man. Both were by turn sulky, animated then veering towards tears. Billy could understand that behaviour from the young lad, but Colin? He was just a waste of space as far as Billy was concerned. His bleating and sweating irritating Billy more than it would normally do. But these weren't normal circumstances. They were shut in a small metal capsule, in close proximity to each other, which served to highlight each person's foibles and habits.

The passengers had been allowed to relax a little more, certainly in terms of movement. It seemed their captors had acknowledged that they were in it for the long haul and were finding it too hard to keep everyone quiet and stop them moving around. Shouting was losing its effect, but not the guns. So a while ago Kourash had told the hostages his name and said that they could move around the carriage, change seats and chat between themselves if they wanted to.

David, Charlie's dad, had requested permission to get a pack of cards out of his rucksack. He hadn't been allowed to get them himself, but one of the hijackers had found them and for a while, at least, Charlie had been distracted by playing card games.

However, it was now getting dark and becoming cold and Charlie had starting asking for his Mum and wanting to know when they could go home. As his sulky anger turned to tears, Peggy had moved over to comfort him. The fact that Charlie let her, Billy believed, was an indication of how scared he was. So Peggy and Charlie were cuddled up together under a blanket Peggy had remembered was in the driver's cab. An old travelling rug, just one of the many items regularly left behind by distracted passengers.

None of the hijackers appeared to speak English, apart from Kourash, although they could be pretending not to, of course. It was difficult to say. So the next time Kourash himself came through the carriage Billy stood and blocked his passage.

For a moment, neither moved. Silently gauging each other's reaction. Kourash's grip tightened on his gun as he pointed it at Billy's stomach.

"What is it this time?" Kourash said. "What do you want now? I've let you move about, get things to amuse the kid and handed out bottles of water. What else is there, apart from letting you go, that is, which is something that isn't going to happen I can assure you."

"We think it's only fair you tell us what's happening. How long you think we're going to be kept here. What demands you've made of the authorities."

"Now look here, Billy," interrupted Colin. "There's no need to antagonise the bloke," his voice rising an octave at the end of his sentence. "Sit down," said Colin and pawed at Billy's jacket.

Ignoring the pathetic Colin, Billy remained where he was, hoping the determination in his gaze would make Kourash realise Billy wouldn't move until he got some answers.

"It's not an unreasonable request," Billy said. "If this is going to take some days to sort out, you're going to have to arrange for food and water to be brought to the train. So far we've had nothing to eat and very little to drink and if you're not careful you're going to have medical problems on your hands. Hazel here is pregnant and Colin already looks like he's a prime candidate for a heart attack."

"Now look here," Colin repeated what was fast becoming his very annoying mantra, but Kourash dismissed Colin's interruption by swinging the gun in his direction. Colin took the hint and fell silent, once again mopping his sweaty face with a hanky that was as wet as the surface he was patting.

"Days?" said Mick. "Who said anything about days?"

"Jesus," David joined in. "Do you think we'll really be here that long?"

"I've got medical appointments to attend!" squeaked Hazel, who up until that point had mostly kept herself occupied with knitting a baby blanket, that she had proudly shown to the others.

"See, Kourash," Billy said. "We've all got lives to lead and we want to get back to them."

"And you?" he asked Billy. "What's your life? You look quite athletic and seem to be the group's natural leader. Always asking questions. Always organising."

But Billy was ready for Kourash's probing. He'd known questions would come sooner or later. Had seen the hijackers look at him suspiciously from time to time, when they thought he couldn't see them. Billy had tried not to stand out, but realised that was impossible. He was the tallest and most well built of all the passengers and try as he might, there was no disguising his natural wish to take command.

"Let me see," Kourash continued, "Police? Army? Bodyguard?"

"That's a laugh," Billy said. "Although I have been a bouncer at my local boozer," Billy replied truthfully. "But these days I'm a personal trainer."

"Really?" Kourash regarded Billy closely. "I suppose that would explain the muscles."

"And the bossiness," said Billy. "In my line of work I'm used to people doing what I tell them to."

Sticking as close to the truth as possible made it easier for Billy to hide the lies. Wanting to detract Kourash from questions about his background, Billy asked again, "So, what about food and drink?"

"On its way. If you'll let me pass I'm going to supervise the transfer. I take it you all like pizza? And there should be hot coffee and tea."

"Yeah, pizza," called Charlie. "I can have some can't I, dad?"

"Yes, of course you can," his father replied, hugging Charlie.

Billy looked at the passengers and saw the relief on their faces and the anticipation of hot food and drink.

"Emma," Kourash shouted, "Come with me."

"Why, what have I done?" she said, looking around at the others, her eyes begging them for support.

"Nothing," Kourash replied, pushing Billy out of the way and dragging Emma to her feet. Holding the gun to her head, he said, "It's just that I told the authorities that if they try anything stupid, like storming the train when they bring the food, then I'll shoot a hostage. And you will do nicely."

19:00 hours

Everything was ready. Food, water and hot drinks had been loaded onto a small maintenance vehicle, which was standing on the tracks, outside the Ribblehead station. The instructions from Kourash had been that only civilians must deliver supplies to the train. No one armed, or in uniform allowed, or a hostage would be shot. Any funny business and a hostage would be shot. Any attempt by snipers to kill one of the hijackers during the transfer and a hostage would be shot. The repetition of the rules were beginning to get on Crane's nerves. He got it. Do anything stupid and a hostage would be shot.

Keane had been given 24 hours by Kourash, to get approval from the British and Afghan authorities to start releasing some prisoners. Nine of those hours had already gone and Crane knew they were no nearer to agreeing to the hijacker's demands.

Crane had been part of the heated video conference meeting, when the men in charge couldn't even agree that they should let the British diplomats at the Embassy in Kabul contact the Afghan President. What was the point, some argued. No one was going to make the decision to agree to the demands. Britain had a 'no negotiation with terrorists' policy and that wasn't about to change. Not even to save the lives of innocent members of the British public.

Mike Keane's mission, therefore, was to get as much information on the hijackers and hostages that he could. Negotiate small acts of kindness for the hostages, such as the food that would shortly be ferried out to them. And barter as hard as he could for the release of as many as he could. Not an enviable job. Not one that Crane would want. He would be more than likely to shout and swear at the bloody hijackers, than accept their demands and meekly turn the other cheek.

In the meantime, the upper echelons of the military command were working out the best way and time to storm the train. Crane knew that was the only way this was going to end. But would it work? Would it be the best solution? By the time the smoke cleared from the attack, who would be left alive? His biggest fear was that Billy wouldn't make it.

"Crane!" someone shouted. He took a deep breath and turned around to see Mike Keane standing on the platform. Crane walked towards him.

"We're ready," Keane said. "Are you sure you and Dudley-Jones want to do this?"

"Well, I can only speak for myself and I'm ready. I couldn't let anyone else go. I need to see with my own eyes what's going on. And Dudley-Jones there," Crane indicated the young man shivering slightly in his shirt sleeves, "might just recognise someone, which would help with his intelligence gathering."

"Very well. I can't come for obvious reasons. Can't have Kourash recognising my voice. I have to stay distant and unidentified. A faceless negotiator trying to gain his trust is better than a negotiator turning up to talk to him face to face when he least expects it. Anyway, the others are on the maintenance vehicle, so I'll let you go. Good luck," and with a nod of his head he moved back inside the station to phone and tell Kourash the food was on its way.

Crane and Dudley-Jones climbed into the back of the vehicle, which was an extended pick-up truck, with space for a driver and three passengers to sit inside and an open rear cargo area. By the front and rear tyres were small rollers clamped to the track. The Northern Rail employee who was driving was doing a fair job of not looking afraid, although Crane could see he had the steering wheel in a vice-like grip and kept swallowing. A lot. The plan was for the driver to stay in the vehicle and for the other three to jump out and carry the food and drink along the small pathway next to the track to the waiting hijackers, who would accept it at the door of the driver's cab.

Crane tried not to think of the 100 foot drop as they crawled along the viaduct in the dark, the truck headlights crazily illuminating parts of the Yorkshire Dales as they swung around the arc of the viaduct. The press pack was swept by the headlights for a short moment and Crane felt the eyes of the world on him. All the major television stations were now in place, relentlessly showing live news feeds from their reporters in situ. Luckily Crane hadn't told his wife Tina what he was doing. He knew she would be glued to the television along with the rest of the nation, indeed the rest of the world. She knew he was up in Yorkshire, knew Billy was on the train, but didn't know the extent of Crane's involvement in the negotiations.

Crane and his men wore open necked shirts and

trousers, having been made to take off their ties and belts. He could understand that it was less likely they could conceal weapons in that type of attire, but it made for a bloody cold and uncomfortable journey. By the time they arrived at the hijacked train, the hairs on his arms were standing on end and full of goose bumps. But whether the reaction was from cold or fear, Crane didn't want to call it, so settled for a bit of both.

Upon their arrival at the train, Crane and Dudley-Jones slid out of the truck and walked round to the back. They were met by another soldier, Frank Potts, who was one of the sentries at Ribblehead Station and had volunteered to help.

Crane nodded at the two men accompanying him as they stood at the back of the pick-up, arms full, and started to lead the way. The weather was being kind and although cold, there was only the hint of a breeze, not enough to ruffle Crane's short black hair. He had to resist the need to scratch the scar on his face, more concerned with not dropping the pizzas he was carrying, than he was with relieving the irritation. But all the same, it stood as a reminder that things weren't always what they seemed to be. The IED in Afghanistan that had contained shrapnel which had slashed into his face had come out of no-where and he needed to be alert, just in case this mission went wrong as well.

The headlamps of the truck illuminated the path as the three men walked past it, towards the train. The truck had stopped just a few yards short, so there wasn't far to walk, thank goodness. Crane's arms were full of pizza boxes, Dudley-Jones struggled under the weight of four large water containers and Potts had four large industrial sized thermos flasks full of tea and coffee. Crane could see the windows on the train driver's cab were covered by blinds, or paper, as they approached it. Whatever it was, it stopped Crane and his men seeing inside. All they could see were vague shapes behind the protective black out. As Crane passed the front of the train, the cab door was flung open, spotlighting young girl stood in the doorway, with a gun pointed at her head.

19:15 hours

Kourash looked at the three men standing by the side of the train, all looking slightly stupid in their thin attire, just as he asked. His aim was to put them on the wrong foot, make them feel disadvantaged, so they would be more than likely to do as they were told. It would appear it had worked. Two of them looked decidedly uncomfortable, but not the man in the lead. That man had an arrogance about him. No, not arrogance, Kourash decided, looking at him closely. More a belief in himself. Their eyes met and the man didn't flinch or look away, coolly meeting his gaze, until it was Kourash himself who dropped his eyes first.

"Name," Kourash demanded, recovering.

"Crane, Tom Crane."

"Less of the James Bond, please. This is reality, not some film set. Now, I'm going to move backwards and take this lovely young girl with me. My compatriots will come and take the supplies from you. Good behaviour means Emma here will live. Bad behaviour... well I think you get the picture."

Crane and the other two with him nodded their agreement and Kourash walked backwards, dragging

Emma with him by her hair, as two of his friends moved in to take the supplies off the first two men. The supplies were placed on the floor of the cab and then ferried into the body of the train. The pizzas and water transfer went well, but then, as if in slow motion, Kourash saw the third man, who was carrying four large flasks, trip over the rail as he moved towards the cab door. Unable to protect himself with his hands full, he dropped the flasks and put out his hands to break his fall. Recovering from his stumble, the man started to straighten and put a hand in his pocket.

As Kourash watched, the man pulled something out of his trouser pocket. Kourash instinctively reacted to the threat by swinging his gun around. Away from Emma. Towards the head of the third man.

"Potts, no!" called Crane.

But Potts continued to pull something out of his pocket. Leaving Kourash with no choice but to pull the trigger. As Potts fell, the sound of the gunshot rumbled and echoed around the valley like thunder.

"No!" Crane shouted.

Emma put her hands over her ears and began screaming.

As Kourash's men jumped down to recover the flasks of hot drink, Crane screamed, "You fucking bastard. He was only pulling out his handkerchief," and Kourash turned to see a strip of white material hanging out of the man's trouser pocket.

"I don't care," Kourash replied. "You were warned what would happen if anything went wrong. You're lucky I didn't kill young Emma here." He turned to her. "Stop screaming you stupid bitch," he said and letting go of her hair, slapped her across the face.

Emma fell to the floor, then half crawled, half

stumbled out of the cab and disappeared back into the carriage.

Crane and Dudley-Jones watched as the cab door was slammed shut in their faces. That seemed to break their mesmerisation and they immediately turned to Potts. Squatting down beside the fallen man, Crane placed his hand on Potts' neck and was relieved to feel a pulse.

"He's alive, get his feet," he shouted to Dudley-Jones and together they carried the injured man back to the vehicle. Slinging him onto the cab bed, they jumped up beside him and Crane banged his hand on the driver's roof. The man took the hint and after a couple of unexpected jerks, the truck drove steadily backwards, towards the safety of the station.

"He's been shot in the shoulder above the heart," Crane said to Dudley Jones, as he ripped off his white shirt. "Here, make a compression pad out of this and hold it against the wound. He's losing a lot of blood, the bloody stuff's everywhere." As Dudley-Jones obeyed the instruction, Crane looked back towards the train and thought about what he'd seen.

It didn't take long before they arrived back at the station and helping hands took Potts from them and loaded him onto a stretcher. As a paramedic took over holding the compression pad from Dudley-Jones, he asked, "Are you hurt, sir?"

"What?"

"You're covered in blood. Is it yours?"

Dudley-Jones looked down at his once pristine shirt and shook his head. "No, no it's not," he said and turned and walked into the station. His face was drained of colour, as if his blood had drained out of it and poured onto his shirt.

Crane walked to the front of the vehicle. The driver was still sat there with the door closed. Crane opened it and looked at the frozen man inside. His face was glazed with sweat and his eyes blank from shock.

"Come on," Crane said. "Let's get you out of there."

The driver turned to his head to look at Crane.

"My hands," he said. "I can't move them."

Crane reached out and unprized the man's fingers, one by one, then helped the driver out of his seat and continued to hold him up as they walked together along the platform, towards a waiting ambulance.

Once the driver had been delivered to the paramedics for treatment for shock, Crane turned away to find Mike Keane standing in front of him.

"What the fuck happened, Crane?"

"Now hang on," Crane immediately bridled at the man's language and tone of voice.

"How can you get delivering supplies wrong, eh? What did Potts do to get himself shot?"

"Nothing, Keane. He didn't do anything wrong. He just fell, that's all."

"That's all? There has to have been more to it than that!"

"Oh, so whatever went wrong is our fault, is that what you're trying to say? Or have you forgotten you're dealing with a terrorist, Keane? A nut job who thinks he can take on the British government and win."

Keane took a few deep breaths. "Okay, let's say Kourash over-reacted. But the question is, what did he over-react to? What did that bloody idiot do?"

"From what I could see, he fell because he'd tripped over the railway line and then as he got up, he went to take his handkerchief out of his pocket."

"His handkerchief? You have to be joking."

"No I'm not. He must have wanted to wipe his hands clean."

"Jesus H Christ," Keane shook his head. "At least Kourash didn't shoot to kill."

"Actually, I've been thinking about that," Crane said as they walked back to the command centre, their anger dissipating as they once again focused on the hostage situation. "I don't think he deliberately shot Potts in the shoulder. I don't think he's a very good shot. He could have been trying for his heart."

"Really? Interesting."

"I saw his hand briefly wobble before he squeezed the trigger," continued Crane. "It was just a moment's hesitation, but I don't think he's shot anyone before. At least if he has, not at such close range."

"Are you thinking what I'm thinking?" Keane mused.

"Yep. Maybe they're not military trained. They could be more a band of brothers who have come together to get their families released, just like Kourash said. That makes them vulnerable."

"And makes our job easier."

"Well, the job of the lads who eventually go in, yes. It makes their job easier."

"On the other hand..." Keane stopped and looked at Crane. "It makes them more likely to react impulsively. Means they're more volatile."

"Which puts the hostages in greater danger," Crane said.

19:20 hours

As the smell of pizza permeated the carriage, the hostage's spirits lifted and their mouths filled with saliva. Billy smiled at the look of anticipation on Charlie's face. The young boy's upset at wanting to go home to his mum, temporarily forgotten. Two of the hijackers passed around the pizza boxes, one per two people, with instructions that the remaining boxes were to be held over for breakfast.

"Yeah," laughed Charlie. "Pizza for tea and for breakfast!" causing his father to smile indulgently.

Billy had a piece of pizza half way to his mouth, looking forward to it as though it were his favourite meal of steak and chips, when the gunshot echoed through the carriage. It immediately dispelled the upbeat mood that had spread amongst the hostages.

Peggy and Hazel screamed, with Peggy calling out, "Emma! Emma!"

Mick took one look at Billy, then putting his arms around Peggy, he turned her away from the slight of Emma tumbling through the door.

Billy, though, didn't have the luxury of doing nothing, as he was the self appointed champion of the hostages. So he rose out of his seat and grabbed Emma as she emerged from the driver's cab. Pulling her to her feet, he quickly ran his hands along her arms and legs, to check for wounds. Her face and top were covered in blood, so he asked, "Emma, is that your blood? Are you hurt?" He thought she was okay, but needed to hear it from her.

"No, no," she gulped, "I'm okay, it's the other man."

Guiding her to a seat and asking Mick to get some water for her, Billy sat next to her and said, "Emma, can you tell me what happened?"

"One of the men bringing the stuff fell and the next thing I knew Kourash fired his gun. There, was, um, blood everywhere. Did he kill him? Billy, what are we going to do? He's going to kill us all!"

Emma's voice had risen hysterically and Billy held her close in an attempt to stop her cries, which were upsetting the others in the carriage.

"Shhh," he soothed. "It'll be alright. We'll get out, just you wait and see."

"Do you think so?"

"Definitely." He was quite enjoying the sensation of having Emma in his arms, so decided to try and keep her there for a little longer.

"What do you do, Emma?" he asked, hoping to distract her from her fear and shock.

"What?"

"What do you do? Where do you work?"

"Oh, I'm a student, English literature." Emma was calming down, her breathing becoming more regular.

"Ah, so that's why you read so much."

"Um, suppose so."

"And look so bookish," Billy teased.

"Oy, you," she pushed herself upright. "Do I really?"

"Afraid so. I think it's the glasses."

"I'll have you know they're very fashionable," she said and pushed them up her nose indignantly, but the corner of her mouth had started to go up in a lopsided smile. Until she tried to see through the glasses. She ripped them off her face and handed them to Billy.

"They're, um, its his, oh shit," and unable to keep her emotions in check anymore, she began to cry.

Billy looked over at Peggy, who was quickly becoming a mother figure among them and she got out of her seat, walked over to Emma, put her arms around the young girl and helped her from her seat.

"Come on, love, let's get you cleaned up." Turning to the hijacker standing guard over them and positioned at the toilet door, she said, "We need to go in there."

The man looked Emma up and down before he nodded his head and moved out of the way of the door.

As Peggy ran water in the sink, Kourash returned to the carriage. The remaining passengers looked at him and it was as if they collectively held their breath. It was Hazel who broke the silence.

"Emma needs a change of clothes. I've got a spare top in my bag. I'm going to get it for her," and she stood, arching her back and placing a hand on it as she stood, her swollen belly pushed forward. Billy noticed she hadn't asked Kourash for permission, but told him. Perhaps there was some backbone in the hostages after all.

Hazel pushed her way out of the seats and stood in front of Kourash. Billy watched the stand-off, wondering what Kourash would do. As he moved out of the way, Billy wondered if the fact that he had just backed down was a sign of weakness. Maybe. It could be Hazel's pregnancy, just respect for her condition. But studying Kourash, Billy could see the gun tremble slightly in his hand and hoped to God it wasn't out of fear. Fear made people unpredictable and prone to do stupid things.

"Come on, everyone, let's eat," Billy called. "No point in letting the pizza go cold and we need to keep our strength and spirits up."

As everyone nodded in agreement and once more lifted the food to their mouths, Kourash turned away and walked back into the driver's cab. One to us, Billy thought. A small triumph, but a triumph all the same.

20:00 hours

The gunshot had stirred up a different hornet's nest. That of the press pack. There was no dismissing the noise as a car backfiring. No point in denying that what everyone had heard was a gunshot. So the authorities didn't. But they did ask the press for their discretion when it came to the hapless soldier that had been shot. No one was to name him, or even try and find out his name. He was recovering in hospital and that's all they were to report. It was an unfortunate mishap. Failure to comply would result in the newspaper or television crew being barred from the press area and from any further press briefings. Faced with that sort of determination, they had no option but to comply. So it was a rather muted Harry Poole and Diane Chambers who left the briefing.

After receiving the cryptic message from Crane earlier in the day that she should find Harry Poole, she had done as he'd asked and was delighted with the outcome of the meeting. Harry had said that if she left Billy's name out of her stories, he would help further her career and give her valuable experience. At first she'd been sceptical, as Crane had blindsided her on more than one occasion. But it seemed Harry Poole was a pretty straight guy, or if not completely straight, pretty bloody persuasive.

"I'm happy to have you work with me," he'd said. "But I run the show and you do as you're told. I write the day and night leads, concentrating on any interviews and the news conferences in and around the press centre. Oh, and I edit everything you write and have the final sign-off."

"What exactly am I to write then, if you're doing all that?"

"You're to go out and get me as many sidebars and features as you can. I want plenty of facts and colour. I want to know all about the hostages - apart from Billy, of course. He's out of bounds. I want details of Bagram Detention Centre. I want to be able to feel I'm in there, walking around. I need the sights, sounds and colour of the place. I want background on President Karzia and the line that he and the Afghan Government are taking on the prison and the prisoners in it. I also want any other hostage situations that we can compare this one with. How did they turn out? What were the outcomes? How many survived? I think that lot should keep you occupied for now."

Diane had tried very hard not to show her pleasure and excitement and had bitten the insides of her cheeks to stop the grin threatening to spread across her face. Adopting a casual attitude she'd then said, "And what about when they storm the train? Where will I be then?"

Harry had stood considering her for a moment. "Then you can be with me, on the front line nearest the train. We'll write that one together."

"And my by-line?" Diane wasn't going to comply

without confirmation that she would get credit in a national newspaper for her copy.

Harry had nodded, "You'll get credit for the copy you write and for the big article we write together when the army go in."

Resisting the temptation to fling her arms around Harry Poole, especially as he was quite attractive in a rugged, rumpled kind of way, although a bit old for her, she'd merely said, "It's a deal," and held out her hand.

Her scepticism had risen to the fore once again, though, during the press conference they'd just left and once outside she pulled Harry away from the main body of people, for a more private conversation.

"You don't think it was Crane that was shot, do you?" she hissed as she was jostled by people rushing back to reclaim their spots.

"No," replied Harry, "he's too good. Basically they're saying it was just an unfortunate accident that caused a hijacker to over-react. No harm done. It's not going to affect the negotiations."

"That's the official line, at least," said Diane.

"Well, that's all we have to go on."

"Unless you ask Crane," Diane smiled coyly at Harry.

"Ask him what?"

"Ask him what really happened. Ask him if the soldier really survived. Or if the hijackers have claimed their first victim. Sorry, but I just don't buy that happy crap they're trying to feed us. The soldier is doing well, it's just a flesh wound, etc, etc."

"And why would Crane give us that sort of information? If you're right that is."

Harry put his arm out to stop a fellow reporter from running full pelt into Diane.

"Firstly, because we're going along with his plan, so we need some sort of reward," to which Harry laughed. "And secondly," Diane ploughed on, "because we'll feed him what information we can get on the hijackers and trust me, I'm bloody good at my job. And I'm not restricted like the intelligence services are. I've got people up and down the country I can call on, student friends who are now working on local papers, people accepted in the communities and who can get locals talking..."

Harry stopped laughing and stared at her.

"But most importantly of all," Diane crowed, "he can use us to leak information. To help him manipulate public opinion. At the moment the mood of the country is favourable to placating the hijackers and helping the hostages. But what about when they storm the train? Crane and his cronies will need the public behind them before they go in. We can get the good people of Britain baying for blood. Look at the success The Sun has had over the years with their campaigns. We could be the voice of the British people. Whip up support for the soldiers and police to go in and rescue the poor hostages."

Something else whipping up was the wind and Diane pushed her unruly dark hair out of her eyes so she could gauge Harry's reaction.

"But that would mean writing inflammatory articles," he said.

"Precisely," agreed Diane. "Inflammatory articles are my forte and manipulation is Sgt Major Crane's."

21:00 hours

"He's what?" Crane spluttered. He'd just been watching the press conference from the wings, when Dudley-Jones had sidled up to him and whispered in his ear. Crane turned to face Dudley-Jones. "Potts is dead! Are you sure?"

Dudley-Jones looked at Crane as if to say, 'do I look like I'm joking?' "Apparently the bullet nicked an artery. He'd lost too much blood. There was nothing anyone could do."

"Fuck. What happens now I wonder?" and Crane and Dudley-Jones turned away from the press conference, to go back to the waiting room and have a word with Keane.

"Are you going to tell Kourash?" Crane asked Keane without preamble, as he walked into the small shop. Keane was staring out of the window, but Crane guessed he wasn't seeing the view.

"Not sure yet," Keane replied slowly. "My first instinct is to say no. Perhaps use it later as a bargaining tool. What do you think?" Keane turned to face Crane as he asked his question.

"I think I want to smash the bastard's face in, for

killing a soldier who did nothing more than try to pull a handkerchief out of his pocket."

"Not an option, Crane."

Crane took a few deep breaths. "No, I know," he conceded as he calmed down. "I see what you mean. About not telling Kourash yet, that is," and he subconsciously scratched at the scar under his short, cropped beard. "We could use it to try and get something out of him. Why should we trust you when you've killed an innocent man? Is that the sort of thing you're thinking?"

"Something like that. Yes, I think I'll withhold that piece of information for now. Make sure the others know, will you? And we don't want it appearing in the press. At least not yet."

"Will do," and Crane left, glad that Keane was willing to discuss strategy with him. But he didn't stop in the waiting room, but went outside for a cigarette first. As he got his welcome nicotine hit, he sent a text to Billy: *Soldier dead. Not telling anyone for now. Be careful. Shooter volatile.*

Kourash was, indeed, finding it difficult to hold his temper. It wasn't the fact that he'd shot the delivery man that was the problem. It was his fellow hijackers. They were all over him, pushing and jostling, their anger and fear emanating from them like a miasma.

"What do you think you're doing?"

"We agreed - no shooting!"

"You could ruin everything for us."

"They're not going to release any prisoners if we start killing people. This was supposed to be a peaceful protest."

Their voices were raised. They spoke in staccato

sentences. All were babbling at once.

Kourash eventually managed to get a word in, by holding up his hands as a signal for silence. "Alright, you've all made your point," he said. "I made a mistake, okay? I didn't mean to shoot anyone, but the man put his hand in his pocket. I thought he was going to pull out a gun."

"But he wasn't, was he?" one of his colleagues demanded.

"No, but I didn't know that at the time. Anyway I deliberately avoided his heart and his stomach." Kourash became conciliatory. "I'm sorry. I guess the pressure just got to me."

Kourash bowed his head and looked at the floor for a couple of seconds. Then when he thought he done enough to convince them, he continued speaking, raising his head once again to look them in the eyes.

"Anyway, I need to speak to the negotiator again. Make sure he understands that they have only 12 hours left in which to report back with how many prisoners are going to be released."

"What if they refuse to co-operate?"

"Then they already know I'm determined. Because I wasn't afraid to use my gun, they'll now understand that I won't hesitate to shoot a hostage when I threaten to. So, you see, my mistake could be a good thing." He waived his gun around, eyes blazing, a big grin on his face. "Don't you see? Now they're afraid of me!"

As Kourash looked around at his fellow hijackers, he was pleased to see alarm on their faces. It was about time they understood that this wasn't a game. It seemed they were beginning to realise he was their natural leader. And that they also had good reason to be afraid of him. Leaders should rule from a position of strength and Kourash was attaining that position, not only over the negotiator, but also over his fellow comrades. He was the most experienced in these things. He was the one who had been to Syria. He was the one who had been trained. Therefore it was right that they were afraid of him. That way they would do as he asked. The alternative was to be shot for dissent.

Kourash tossed his head at his comrades, lifting his chin, looking down on them, striking a regal pose. Daring them to cross him. When no one did, he turned and left them, returning to the driver's cab, to plan his next move.

21:30 hours

The uncanny thing about the otherwise humdrum train, Crane thought, was its immobility on an otherwise empty track in the middle of a pastoral nowhere. With all the windows covered to conceal its interior from outside observers, Crane could only wonder when tensions between the unseen passengers and their captors would fatefully snap. The hidden implications of the outwardly deserted looking train swirled around it like a poisonous, invisible, pall. The two carriage train remained frozen on the tracks where it normally shuttled to and fro so busily, between Carlisle and Settle. The green pasture around the train had become a no-man's land, in which the unconcerned white puffballs of grazing sheep were the only visibly moving objects.

The normally placid village of Ribblehead in the distance, seethed in the hubbub created by a milling host of outsiders. National and local officials and their aides. Heavily armed police. Soldiers and anti-terror specialists. A horde of advisors, medics, psychiatrists and other support workers. Not to mention scores of inquisitive rubberneckers.

It was the world's top news story, so a large media presence exposed the Ribblehead Viaduct to the gaze of hundreds of millions of unseen television viewers and newspaper readers the world over. Amongst the milling hoards Crane knew that, as much as he hated the media, Harry Poole and his new assistant were just doing their job like everyone else.

Looking at the viaduct, Crane wondered how the Victorian engineers managed to build the massive structure, indeed the whole line, in such hostile terrain. He knew that vast numbers of navvies were needed to bore tunnels and build the viaducts in very difficult conditions, resulting in a high death toll. Crane was determined that the hijackers wouldn't add to that number.

With a sigh, he threw away his burned down cigarette butt, scratched at his scar one last time and strode back to the station building, just in time for another briefing from Downing Street.

It wasn't good news for the hostages. COBRA (the crisis response committee set up to coordinate the actions of bodies within the United Kingdom in response to instances of national or regional crisis) had met and agreed that they would not make a deal with the hijackers.

"Well, that's just great," Crane said. "The 24 hour time limit is up tomorrow morning. What the hell are we supposed to do? Kourash is threatening to kill a hostage if we don't meet his deadline and start releasing prisoners. At the moment we're deaf and blind as far as what's going on in the train is concerned. And Kourash is making us look like dumb fucks."

"Now, Crane, that's not strictly true," countered Colonel Booth. "As you well know we've got a drone up in the skies, making sweeps along the length of the train. We have cameras and directional microphones set up - although I have to admit they're a bit too far out to do any good at the moment. However, a satellite is being moved into position and should be on line in the next hour and we'll have 'ears' from later tonight. Plus we have the 'button cameras' that you wear when you take the supplies to the train. So I don't think over-reacting is going to do any good, do you Sgt Major?"

Ignoring Booth, even though Crane had to concede he had a point, Crane turned on the negotiator, demanding, "What the hell are you going to do now, Keane?"

After a pause, Keane said, "We're due to send in more supplies."

"This late at night?"

"Yes. Kourash demanded more water, washing things for the hostages, toilet rolls..."

"Alright, I don't need an inventory. What's your point?"

"If you'll let me speak and stop interrupting," Keane glowered at Crane, "I propose we get some religious leaders to take the supplies this time. When they're there they could try and talk to Kourash. See if they can make him understand that this is a futile endeavour and persuade him and the other hijackers to give themselves up. Now. There must be something in the Qur'an that they can quote about not killing people. We've got two or three Imams back at Dent Station. They've been acting as liaison with the Muslim community and giving specialist advice as required. So it shouldn't take too long to get them here. I'm sure they'll do their bit to help."

Crane looked around the room. Andrew Hardwick

had hope in his eyes, as did the Colonel. But as Crane caught the eye of Dudley-Jones, the look that passed between them said it all. If anyone believed that load of bullshit, then they were just plain stupid. Crane shrugged at the army intelligence operative and said out loud, "I guess if nothing else it could buy us some time."

But in the end it didn't even buy some time. Hanging their heads in shame, the religious leaders registered complete deadlock, on their return from the train. Kourash wouldn't budge in his demands and he took absolutely no notice of their desire for him to give himself up peacefully and let the hostages go. It was beyond their understanding, they said, how a devout Muslim could take this stance. He must have been radicalised. They could do no more than wash their collective hands of him. They shook their heads in dismay and departed.

Crane had no sooner closed the door on them, when the phone from the train rang. Keane ran into the shop to answer it. Crane stayed in the waiting room and listened in the company of Booth, Hardwick and Dudley-Jones.

"You have a lot to answer for, Keane," Kourash shouted as soon as the receiver was lifted.

Crane winced as he heard the anger in Kourash's voice spewing out of the speakers.

"I can't believe you sent in Imams to spout religious rhetoric at me! How dare they tell me what's in the Qur'an? I know perfectly well what is written in that Holy book. They asked me not to take the lives of the hostages, as it is against our religion. Do you know what I said to that?" But Kourash pressed on with his verbal diatribe, not waiting for a reply from Keane. "I said that in that case Bagram Detention Centre should be closed down as it is nothing more than a place for legalised murder. So, that's my new demand. Forget about releasing our families. Shut the whole place down and release everyone! You have less than 11hours. By the time I wake up tomorrow morning, I want to hear that you are meeting my demands. If not, it will be the last sunrise one of the hostages will ever see."

The line went dead and Crane walked though to the shop. He watched Keane slowly replace the receiver and slump down on his desk, bowed down by the responsibility of his unenviable task.

.

23:00 hours

Billy was having trouble sleeping. Not so much from the cramped conditions, but from worry. The last message he'd managed to send to Crane said, *What the f* did you do to K? Very volatile. Possibly no training just fervour.* He didn't know if it would help. He didn't know what would help, if he was honest. Also he had a problem with his mobile. The battery was running low. He was now turning it off between messages as he needed to conserve the power. He considered it was more important that Crane could send him updates, rather than the other way around. For Billy needed advance notice of any attack. He was sure one would come. But when? And how? And when it did come, would he be able to protect the hostages in the chaos? He started to run through some ideas in his head. Helicopters. SAS. Stun grenades. He fantasised about grabbing a gun and putting a bullet through Kourash's head, the man's eyes widening in surprise. Saw that they were still frozen open as Kourash died. Watched as his body crumpled and hit the ground.

As Billy shifted his legs to get comfortable, he thought he heard something. Just the slightest crunch.

He looked around the carriage as best he could without moving and was pretty convinced everyone was asleep. Maybe it had just been someone stirring in a dream. He then imagined he felt the slightest vibration from the floor underneath his feet and smiled to himself. What was happening that he couldn't see? Could there be stealthy, black clad SAS soldiers silently making their way underneath the train, fitting transmitters to the floor of the carriages? If so, from now on Crane and whoever else was part of the crisis team would, if nothing else, be able to hear what was being said in the train.

Billy's thoughts grabbed hold of those gossamer threads of slim hope. The idea that someone was on his side and possibly making advance preparations for a rescue mission, This expectation allowed Billy to close his eyes and manage to sleep. It silenced his rambling, erratic thoughts, as overhead, silent and unobserved, an unmanned drone made yet another sweep of the train.

23:30 hours

"Right, everyone," the Colonel called the meeting to order. This is what we've got so far," and he outlined the fact that they now had microphones in place under each carriage and the driver's cab. The drone had been sweeping the area steadily for the past 12 hours and thermal imaging seemed to confirm that there were fourteen people onboard the train. He also confirmed that plans were being drawn up for a rescue mission. The Prime Minister and the Chiefs of Staff Committee, would have three or four different options for consideration, each dependent upon different elements, such as time of day or night, weather and point of entry.

Crane tried hard to concentrate on Booth's voice, which droned on with no noticeable distinction in modulation. But it was very late and a lot had happened in the last 13 hours. Whilst not wanting to leave the waiting room in case something happened, Crane knew he would have to grab a few hours sleep soon. The plan was that the Colonel would be staying upstairs in the Caretaker's flat, whilst the others were to nip down to the Station Master's House, which had been restored and was now a guest house, to grab a few hours kip. They were to do this on a rota basis, so there would be one of them in the control centre at all times. Keane was to have any calls from Kourash that might come in whilst the somewhat dispirited negotiator was trying to get some well earned rest, patched through to his mobile.

Crane jerked back to the here and now as Booth finished his summing up and turned towards Dudley-Jones. "Any news about the hijackers?" he asked.

"Yes, sir," the Army Intelligence operative replied. "As you know, CCTV captured good images of the hijackers at Dent Railway Station. We saw pictures of them earlier, but didn't know who was who. So far facial recognition has identified one of them as Kourash Abdali," and Dudley Jones brought up the man's image on a large screen that had been installed and hung on one of the walls.

As the picture flashed up, Crane said, "That's the one who seemed to be the leader when we were delivering the food. The one that shot Potts."

"What's his background?" the Colonel asked.

"Surprisingly normal," Dudley-Jones replied. "He was born in Afghanistan, but brought over to England to live with his uncle and aunt as a young boy. He settled here with them, attending school and quickly learning English. The family as a whole were regular members of their local Mosque and Kourash went to extra lessons learning the Qu'ran, as do most Muslim boys. He was a successful student and went to university where he obtained a degree in Politics."

"So what happened to radicalise him, do you think?" Crane asked.

Dudley-Jones said, "Well, it seems that he went to

Syria for a while, to help with the conflict over there, which is where we think he was radicalised. There are rumours that his brother, who still lives in Afghanistan with his parents, was arrested and taken to Bagram Detention Centre, but we're trying to confirm that."

"So we're dealing with someone who is intelligent, has studied politics, studied the Qu'ran and been to Syria. Those four elements seem to have collided to produce the volatile young man we are now dealing with," said Keane, seemingly with a new respect in his voice for Kourash.

"Does that make your job easier or harder?" Crane asked. "Knowing his background?"

"Definitely easier I would say. It gives me a few cards up my sleeve as it were. I can use the knowledge that he would have learned about politics, to try and make him see reality. See the futility of his mission."

"Good luck with that," said Crane, who didn't believe negotiation would work and was fantasising about a rescue mission. Wanting to get Billy and the hostages off the train as soon as possible. But, on reflection, maybe he was being unfair to Keane. Dismissing his ability to get everyone out safely. It was all so bloody confusing.

"We've got people out interviewing his immediate family to see what else we can glean about him. And people are on the ground in Afghanistan doing the same thing," said Dudley-Jones. The young man was the collection point and mouth-piece for all the intelligence being gathered by various agencies.

"Good work," said the Colonel, rather begrudgingly Crane thought, although it could just be the futility of their task, Crane reasoned.

No one was particularly upbeat at the moment.

Tiredness made their brains sluggish and mouths prone to procrastination. The inability to make decisions plaguing all of them. Fatigue pulling at their limbs and wrapping its tentacles around their minds.

The waiting room of the station wasn't an ideal space to work in. The solid stone walls seemed permanently cold to the touch. Heaters had been brought in, but they just served to make everyone sleepy. The cold rarefied air of the Yorkshire Dales being more conducive to brain function. The high ceilings amplified their voices, the sound bouncing off the walls. Their frustrated tones reverberated around the space, making them sound harsher than intended.

"Hardwick and I had better update the Prime Minister, I suppose," Booth said, his face showing his reluctance for the task. "Tell him who we're dealing with. Let me know when you get anything on the other hijackers," and the Colonel nodded to them, then left the room with the civilian co-ordinator.

Crane, Dudley-Jones and Keane listened to the heavy footfalls as the two men made their way to the Caretaker's flat above them, where a secure line to Downing Street had been installed. To Cane's exhausted mind, their feet were drumming a tattoo of defeat.

24:00 hours

"I wanted to apologise, Emma," Kourash said to her, after she'd been taken to the driver's cab and the hijacker that had delivered her had left them alone. The two of them took up most of the confined space as they stood facing each other.

"Apologise? What for? For shooting that man? Or for taking us in the first place?" Emma glared defiantly at him. Arms folded. Her eyes huge behind her glasses. Rays of light from the overhead bulbs glinted off them.

"Both, I guess."

Kourash held her gaze, but Emma couldn't see any remorse written in his eyes. If anything they were alive, dancing as though with amusement. Amused by her anger? That thought made her even more angry. She clenched her fists, wanting to strike him, but not daring to.

"Tell me," he said, "what is it you do? Do you work?"

"No, I'm a student," she replied. "What of it?" and lifted her head higher in defiance. She was still uncertain as to his intentions and rather thrown by this sudden change of subject.

"Of what?"

"English."

"Ah," he smiled, "you study all those great English writers? Who are you studying at the moment?"

"An American writer, actually," she replied. "Truman Capote." Still not sure that she wanted to get into a conversation with him, she kept her answers short and to the point.

"Which book? Breakfast at Tiffany's?"

"No. Although that's the work people tend to think of when you mention Truman Capote. Breakfast at Tiffany's is not a book, it's a short story, or novella, whichever term you prefer." She couldn't resist putting him right and then, caught up in her favourite occupation, which was discussing literature, she said, "Would you believe it if I told you we're currently studying Truman Capote's book, 'In Cold Blood'. It's a true crime account of two young men, who go to steal money from a house and end up going on a killing spree."

Kourash nodded his head slowly, "Pretty ironic choice of reading material for this situation, don't you think? Tell me, what do you make of them?"

"I'm sorry?"

"Smith and Hicock," he said. "Here sit in the driver's seat, it will be more comfortable than standing."

"You mean you've read the book?" Emma tried to evaluate that piece of imparted information as she sat down, the chair creaking and bouncing as she got herself comfortable. Kourash sat cross legged on the floor facing the chair.

"Of course. I was born and educated in England,

just like you," he said. "Friends of mine at university were studying the book, so I read it on their recommendation. Anyway, you've not answered my question. What do you make of them?"

And much to Emma's astonishment, she began to relax as they discussed one of the greatest true crime novels ever written. At least it was in her opinion and in the opinion of millions of other people.

Kourash never seemed to take his eyes off her face as they argued back and forth. Kourash, naturally, was trying to justify the killers' actions and Emma took the opposite stance. He became animated at one point in their discussion and jumped to his feet, pacing around the small space, gesticulating with his hands, imploring her to see his point of view. His black curls bounced off his shoulders and Emma found herself being drawn to this unusual young man. She was trying to compare the man in front of her, someone who wouldn't have been out of place in her university classes, with the person who a few hours ago had shot and wounded an innocent man.

Then, abruptly, Kourash held out his hand and helped her to her feet.

"It's time you got some rest," he said. "Perhaps we can continue this discussion another time." As he talked, he stepped just that bit too close to her. Invaded her personal space. But Emma found that for once she didn't mind. She'd seen a side of Kourash she had never expected and begrudgingly found herself smiling back at him.

Once back in the carriage, as she slipped into her seat, Billy opened his eyes and looked straight at her.

"Where have you been?" he hissed.

"The toilet," Emma replied before she realised what

she'd said. Realised that she'd just lied to Billy.

"That's the other way,"

"What?"

"The toilet is in the opposite direction. Were you in the driver's cab?"

"Don't be stupid, Billy. What would I be doing in there?"

She hoped her reply sounded convincing. The only experience she'd had of lying to someone's face was when she was living at home and her foster parents had confronted her one night, wanting to know where she'd been. She hadn't been a very successful liar then, her foster father seeing right through her masquerade. This time she decided to brazen it out, hoping that her defiance would make Billy believe her.

Seeing his forehead crinkle in consternation, she quickly said, "Anyway I've been hoping to catch you alone. I wanted to know if you thought there was anything we could do to help get ourselves out of this situation."

"Like what?"

"Oh, I don't know, overpower one of the hijackers or something?" and she moved to the seat next to him while they whispered back and forth, trying to think of any way they could escape. But Emma's thoughts weren't really on the ruse she had used to divert Billy's attention. She couldn't seem to take her eyes off the cab door. The door that Kourash was behind.

Day Two
07:00 hours

Dudley-Jones was doing a remarkable job as Intelligence Operative, receiving, consolidating and reporting on the massive amounts of information that was streaming in from various agencies located in other facilities away from the command centre: the Army Intelligence Service; the commanders of the teams responsible for covert surveillance of the train; MI5, MI6, and the police. There simply wasn't sufficient room or buildings or equipment to accommodate everyone at Ribblehead, so they each stayed at their various headquarters. Every new development was flashed up on the screen connected to Dudley-Jones' computer and hard copies stuck onto incident boards, which flanked a whole wall in the station waiting room, which was quickly becoming claustrophobic. Dudley-Jones and Keane wore headsets with microphones, as they were plugged into the communications systems. The other men were sat around the table, which had still not been cleared of the ordnance survey map they had consulted nearly 24 hours ago.

Crane looked around, mindful of the need for

information gathering, but personally more interested in when, where and how a rescue mission would take place.

"Sir!" Dudley-Jones called causing both the Colonel and Crane to respond to the call.

"Well?" demanded the Colonel, who didn't seem to be coping very well with just a few snatched hours of sleep. The man's eyes were rimmed red with fatigue and at times his eyelids seemed so heavy Crane was convinced the man was about to fall asleep. But to be fair Colonel Booth looked no worse than the rest of them. All were crumpled and unkempt, with lines of worry furrowed on their faces.

"What have you got for us this time?"

"The information gleaned from the microphones under the train and the sweeps by the drone, sir," said Dudley-Jones

"Very well, show us," Booth said and everyone turned to look at the screen.

"Basically, the microphones have picked up voices in several parts of the train, which has been confirmed by heat source surveillance from the drone. Unfortunately they aren't picking up much in the way of words, but we can distinguish between male and female voices and occasionally words in different languages."

A model of the train appeared and two figures were placed in the rear carriage.

"Working from right to left, with the front of the train on the left, it appears there are two people in the rear carriage. We presume these are hijackers acting as lookouts. The original black paper they used seems to have been replaced by a film placed on the glass. This means they can see out but we can't see in." Dudley-Jones clicked a key and more figures appeared.

"There are several people milling around in the other carriage and at the moment we can't identify how many are hostages and how many hijackers. However, the intel received from Sgt Williams seems to be confirmed as there are 14 people in total on the train. This would suggest 8 hostages and 6 hijackers as he said, although the movement of people makes it difficult to be precise. We are still working on voice analysis so we know who stays in the carriages and who leaves, which will give us a clearer picture as to who's who."

"And the driver's cab?" asked Crane

"Always at least one person in there as look out, but again that number is fluid. Once again the windows have been filmed over."

"Are the voices in the driver's cabs always male?" asked Keane.

Dudley-Jones frowned for a moment and consulted his screen.

"No, sir, a woman's voice has been heard in the front cab."

"Why did you ask that?" Crane worried at his scar.

"Just trying to ascertain if the hijackers are male or female, Crane. A woman amongst them could be good for us as women are statistically less inclined to commit murder."

"Apart from Rose West and Mira Hindley," mumbled Crane, citing two of Britain's most notorious women serial killers and he turned away to look at the incident boards, not comforted by Keane's statistics at all.

"What about communications?" Crane asked, still looking at the boards. "How are they communicating with the outside world?"

"We believe they are using a secure satellite network to communicate."

"Haven't you blocked it yet?"

"No, sir, we're trying to crack it but no luck as yet." Dudley-Jones looked suitably chastised as Booth glowered at him. But quickly rallying he said, "However, I do have more information on the group of terrorists," and he proceeded to brief the assembled men on their identities and the background information he and his colleagues had gleaned from Facebook and YouTube. They were all of Afghani descent.

"Asa and Farhang were born in the UK. Both are practising Muslims, attending their local mosque, which is one of those on the intelligence services list as being of a high level of concern. Giti and Housyar were born, and lived in, Afghanistan all their lives. They are here on student visas. Mehrab is on MI5's watch list as someone they think could have been radicalised. He had been under surveillance, but as they couldn't see that he'd been plotting anything, they'd cancelled the surveillance a couple of weeks ago. And we already know a lot about Kourash Abdali. Social media is also very active, as you can imagine," Dudley Jones continued.

"Social media?" interrupted the Colonel. "What on earth are you talking about?"

"Mostly Twitter, but also Facebook to a lesser degree."

"Explain."

"Twitter is a community of millions of people around the world. You can send tweets to your followers and also to other people you want to communicate with, but who aren't following you. But you are only allowed to use 140 characters in a tweet.

However, more importantly in our case, are hash tags."

"Hash tags? For God's sake, speak English, or at least in words of one syllable," said Booth and Crane smiled at the confused faces all looking at Dudley-Jones.

"It's a way of drawing the Twitter community together. At the moment there are two main ones that concern us. The first is *#savethehostages* and the other *#supportthehijackers*. These hash tags are used by people in their tweets and help drum up support for their thinking. *#savethehostages* is trending higher than *#supportthehijackers* at the moment, thank goodness. But the point is that these hash tags reflect the popular mood of the people. The team are looking at those Twitter users who are supporting the hijackers."

"Why is that important?" asked the civil servant.

"Well, sir, through that we might find anyone who is actively involved behind the scenes. Someone is feeding them information and as I said earlier, we think it's through a secure satellite link. We are hoping to find the person on the ground who is communicating with them. Twitter users are also trying to sway the mood of the country into backing their cause. Someone somewhere started this hash tag and it's our job to find out who that is."

As Dudley-Jones finished, Crane said, "Well that's all very interesting, and I'm sure there are going to be some red faces in the intelligence services, but what I want to know is - what's going to happen at 10:00 hours? Is President Karzia going to make a statement?"

"No, Crane, he's not," said Hardwick, his voice carrying the weight of the British Government behind his words.

"Well then, if Karzia isn't going to make a statement

or release any prisoners, what is going to happen?"

"From our end?" asked Keane.

"Yes, Keane, from our end." Crane's patience was wearing thin and he struggled to control his temper, so as not to take his frustration out on Keane.

"In that case the answer's easy. Nothing. We're not going to do anything."

The reality of Billy's predicament sliced through Crane. Images of his Sergeant flashed across his closed eyes. Billy on parade. Billy on exercise. He watched Billy creeping around the old cinema; investigating the underneath of the swimming pool in the Garrison Sports Centre; talking to the old Ghurkha, Padam Gurung; trying to help his friend who had been viciously raped.

As he massaged his eyes the images crunched together, leaving just one. The smiling face of Sgt Billy Williams, who Crane was very much afraid he'd never see alive again. There was only one thing to do. So he turned away from the men in the waiting room and walked out into the cool morning air, lighting a cigarette as he went.

08:00 hours

Threading through the crowd, Diane Chambers searched for Harry Poole. As he was tall, she was looking upwards, trying to find his head poking above the sea of people. She'd done it. Found the identity of one of the hijackers. Combined with the exultation of a job well done, was an over-riding sense of relief. She was glad that she had been able to back up her boasts when she'd said her network of contacts would be able to come up with something.

She'd gambled that because the hijackers had joined the train at Dent they probably originated somewhere in the North of England. That way they would have been able to blend into their surroundings, whilst they laid their plans and scouted out a suitable target. She'd bet that not many southerners knew about the Ribblehead Viaduct, whereas here it was a local beauty spot and tourist attraction. So she'd concentrated on the friends who had joined northern provincial papers, with the hope of moving onto something bigger once they'd gained some experience.

Even at university, Diane had recognised the need for a journalist to have good contacts. Everyone she met became someone she could turn to in the future, another notation in her growing address book, which was a vital tool in her ever present pursuit of information. The only thing she'd asked of them was to not print the details until she gave them the go-ahead, mindful of the delicate situation being played out on the train. For once being responsible and respectful rather than gung-ho and headstrong.

Just then the flock of people before her, cleared and she was given a glimpse of the train. She stopped walking and just stood, watching the two carriages. Seeing their vulnerability for the first time, she wondered if that fabricated hulk of metal, plastic and glass would be Billy's salvation or his coffin.

She was startled out of her morbid thoughts by Harry, clapping her on the back.

"Hey, Diane, got you some coffee."

"What? Oh, sorry, thanks."

"Are you alright?" Harry looked down on her, concern on his rugged, weather beaten, vastly more experienced face.

"Yes. Sorry. I was just looking at the train. Got a bit morbid. Just seeing it up there. Isolated. It threw me, that's all." After taking a drink of the hot coffee to revive her, she forced a smile on her face. "You'll never believe what I've got," she said and proceeded to tell him about the information she'd garnered on the hijackers. But she'd left the best until last.

"Wait until you see this," she smiled and clicked a button on her tablet. The media file was an interview with an Afghani couple. They wore western clothes, but the woman had a headscarf covering her hair. They stood upright, as if determined not to be cowed by the interviewer.

Q. Could you tell the viewers who your son is?

A. Kourash Abdali.

Q. Has he always been religious?

A. Yes. He was brought up in the traditional way, went to mosque regularly and studied the Qur'an. We do know that he became obsessed with Islam. We believe he joined various groups and mosques whilst at school and university here in England. This led to him becoming increasingly concerned about the plight of Syrian civilians caught up in the conflict. He'd never been to Syria before but last summer, after he'd graduated, he went there and joined Isis.

Q. Are you talking about the Islamic State in Iraq and the Levant?

A. Yes, that's correct.

Q. Do you realise that of all the rebel groups, Isis is the most brutal? So violent that even Al-Qaeda's leadership has formally distanced itself from them. Do you think they brainwashed him?

A. We think he was convinced by their reasoning, through videos Isis posted on line.

Q. Aren't these used to lure foreign fighters to their cause?

A. We believe he made an informed decision to join them. We strongly deny that he was brainwashed.

Q. So why did he return home?

A. He told us that his brother, who still lives in Afghanistan, had been arrested and detained in Bagram Detention Centre. He said he'd got permission from the Isis leadership to return to England. At the time we thought it was something like compassionate leave, but now it seems he was allowed home in order to strike at the heart of the British Government.

Q. Is Kourash not your biological son?

A. No, he is my brother's son. He was sent to England years ago to give him a better start in life. But just because my wife didn't give birth to him, doesn't mean he is not our son.

Q. And how do you feel about what he is doing?

A. We feel he is doing the honourable thing. He's risking his life to help those oppressed by the British and Americans in his home country of Afghanistan.

The interview finished and the reporter thanked them for their co-operation. Watching the segment again with Harry, Diane noticed that it was the man who answered all the questions, his wife standing meekly by his side. It seemed that despite their western garb, they still adhered to the traditional ways.

"Isn't it fabulous, I've got quite a scoop here," she said and couldn't stop her spreading grin.

"Oh dear. Sorry, Diane, I think you've been had. It's not much of a scoop I'm afraid."

"What? What the hell are you talking about, Harry? My contact assured me no one else had this." Then realisation drained her enthusiasm and after a moment she continued, "It's been sold to someone, hasn't it?"

Harry nodded his agreement.

"Who?"

"Sky News. It's been on the air for the last couple of hours. Sorry."

Diane counted to three to calm herself down. "Oh well," she smiled brightly, "better luck next time, I suppose."

She walked off so that Harry wouldn't see her pink-faced embarrassment. She knew she was playing with the big boys now and had just learned a valuable lesson. Trust no one. Reporting was big business and that interview had just been too valuable. She couldn't really blame her contact for selling it. In all honesty she would probably have done the same thing. So absorbing her disappointment into another layer of her thick skin, she held her head high and strode off to see what else she could find out about the hijackers.

09:00 hours

Crane was wandering through the exhibition centre at the Ribblehead Station. He was intrigued to find that at its height, construction of the Carlisle to Settle railway line employed 7,000 men. Nearly 1,000 of these worked at Ribblehead on the major engineering tasks of building the Ribblehead viaduct and Blea Moor tunnel. The area was bleak and isolated and so accommodation had to be specially built to house this army of workers. Construction camps, or shanty towns, as they were popularly called, grew up around 1870.

Most of the workers lived in prefabricated single-storey wooden terraces, or even large tents, but the Ribblehead settlement also included more substantial buildings such as shops, public houses, a school, post office and library, as well as a small isolation hospital built during a smallpox epidemic.

It reminded Crane of the large army base of Camp Bastion in Afghanistan. At its height it was as large as the town of Reading, providing accommodation and support for thousands of troops. Currently being dismantled and the area once again being returned to desert, Camp Bastion would disappear as effectively as the Ribblehead shanty town disappeared after construction of the viaduct had been completed.

His inspection of the bleak black and white photographs from the era was interrupted by his phone ringing. Eagerly drawing it from his pocket, he saw it was not from Billy, but from his boss, Captain Draper.

"Morning, sir."

"Morning, Crane, any news?" Draper asked, so Crane filled him in on the unsuccessful mission by the Imams late last night.

"So, I take it that now things have settled down somewhat and we're probably in for the long haul, that you'll be returning to Aldershot, to your regular duties."

Crane considered this comment that wasn't quite an order, but a tacit request. Crane wasn't about to fall for that one and had been prepared for just such a move by Draper.

"I'm afraid that won't be possible, sir."

"Why not? What potential role could you have that warrants you staying in the command centre? I realise Billy is still a hostage, but is that sufficient reason for you being part of the team?"

Crane couldn't quite work out if Draper really meant what he was saying, or merely covering his arse. No way was Crane leaving until Billy was freed and both men knew that. Deciding Draper was covering his arse, Crane said, "I understand your concern, sir, but I've been invited to stay. Ordered actually. And I'm sure you don't want me to deliberately disobey a direct order from Colonel Booth, do you?"

"Ah."

"Ah, sir?"

"Well, in that case, carry on, Sgt Major."

"Thank you, sir."

Crane cut the call. Booth, of course, had done no such thing, but Crane doubted anyone would actually ask him to verify the order. In the meantime, Crane had a supply run to make. Keane said it was important that the same faces appeared each time, to make Kourash feel more secure and Crane intended to make one of those faces, his.

10:05 hours

The telephone at Ribblehead Station rang at precisely five minutes past the hour. It was Kourash, of course, Keane knew, as he reluctantly picked up the receiver.

"So, you and your Government have decided to ignore my demands. Why have you not set any prisoners free from Bagram? Why hasn't President Karzia been on the television?"

Kourash's questions tumbled out, his anger a living thing, snaking its way down the railway tracks to Ribblehead Station. Forcing Keane to face his actions, or rather lack of them. Keane did the only thing he could. Answered a question with a question.

"How do you know they haven't been released?"

"Because it would have been on the news by now," Kourash spoke to Keane as though addressing a child.

Keane decided to ignore Kourash's disrespect.

"What news?" he asked. "Do you have radios? Internet? Secure mobile phones?"

"Never mind what we've got, you're fishing and I've no intention of telling you anything. I know that you haven't done as I demanded, so I will carry out my threat and the death of a hostage will be on your head and on the heads of the members of the British Government."

"Kourash, don't," Keane shouted. "Let's talk, perhaps we can work it out," but Keane was talking to a dead line. Kourash had slammed the phone down.

Keane slowly stood, pushing himself up to his full height and walked into the waiting room. Everyone turned to look at him. Their mouths opening and closing as though they were gabbling. But no sound came out. You could have heard a pin drop in the room. Hardwick sat down heavily onto the nearest chair. Dudley-Jones' face was that awful putrid red. The Colonel looked around the assembled team, as though looking for someone to blame. And Crane? Well, Crane appeared to be praying - eyes downcast, hands held together, mumbling something only he could hear.

Keane did the only thing he could. Joined them as they waited for the inevitable.

Kourash stayed in the driver's cab, looking down at the telephone. Still trying to assess what had just happened. He had to face it now. It was time. Time for him to show the British establishment that he meant what he said. That he was serious. He had prayed for this moment for a long time, since receiving the call to do Allah's work. This was his opportunity to make the world aware of the injustice being meted out day after day in Afghanistan by the occupying forces. He held his gun just that little bit tighter, to stop his hands shaking. He could feel the anger building in him. That was good. His anger would be the weapon he would use to carry out his threat.

Flinging open the door of the cab, his eyes swept the hostages and his fellow hijackers. It was clear they all knew there was something wrong. None of them would meet his gaze. It seemed that they could feel it in the air. Tension cracked around him like electricity from a pylon, as he decided who he would take.

Making his choice, Kourash said, "Mick, come with me," and his nearest compatriot reached over, grabbed a handful of Mick's clothing and pulled him to his feet.

"What are you doing?" Billy shouted. "Where are you taking him?"

Mick looked bewildered. He looked first at Billy, then at Kourash. But Kourash ignored the silent plea in the man's eyes and pushed Mick in front of him into the cab.

"For God's sake, leave him alone!" shouted Peggy. "He's done nothing to you! None of us have!"

Charlie squirmed in his father's arms, burrowing his way into David's coat like a rabbit disappearing into a warren, at the first sign of a predator.

Emma stood. "Kourash," she said. "Don't, please don't."

Kourash so very much wanted for all this to be over, but knew the only way to make that happen was to show the authorities strength not weakness. So he turned away from Emma and followed Mick into the driver's cab.

The barrage of protests that followed him from the hostages, were suddenly silenced as Kourash heard his compatriots ready their guns. Training his own gun on Mick and picking up the phone he waited until it was answered.

"Keane," Kourash said. "I've got someone here who wants to talk to you," and he handed the telephone to Mick.

"Tell him your name," Kourash instructed, "and

don't forget to mention the gun I'm holding to your head."

Mick did as he was told and then Kourash grabbed the receiver from the hapless man.

"Goodbye," he said to Keane.

But before replacing the telephone on its cradle, he discharged his weapon.

Crane burst into the shop, following the words he was spewing. "What the fuck just happened, Keane? Has he shot someone? For God's sake, why did you wind him up earlier? Now look what's happened. All because you made him angry."

"Crane, I was just trying to get information out of him."

"Well you failed miserably at that, didn't you? And now it looks like all you've achieved is to endanger the life of one of the hostages! He could very well have shot the bloody train driver!" Crane's anger was like a train itself, thundering towards Keane at full steam. "And I've already told you what I'll do to you if you manage to get Billy shot!"

Keane, as calm as ever said, "It's alright, Crane. The driver is still alive."

"And how the bloody hell do you know that?" Crane sneered, not yet ready to give Keane any dispensation.

Keane pointed to the screen on the desk next to the telephone. It showed the immobile train atop the viaduct. "Because if Kourash really had shot someone, he would have thrown the body out of the train."

10:10 hours

It was as if the gunshot was still reverberating around the carriage. The sound of a weapon going off in such a small space left their ears ringing in its wake. It seemed as though everyone was holding their breath, hostages and hijackers alike. Billy was in shock. What had Kourash just done? Surely he hadn't really shot Mick? The tension in the carriage ratcheted up another notch as they collectively watched the door handle on the driver's cab door, turn. As the door opened, Billy could only see Mick's back as he was pushed out of the door and tumbled to the floor in the aisle of the carriage.

Billy was out of his seat and at Mick's side with one bound. The train driver was still alive. Gibbering incoherently, but alive. After Billy checked him for blood and injuries and finding none, he pulled him up and manoeuvred him into a seat. Mick grabbed at Billy's shirt.

"I thought he was going to kill me! I was convinced I was going to die! What are we going to do?"

But Billy had no answer. All he could do was pat Mick's arm.

The sound of hysterical sobbing reached Billy as his

hearing cleared and he looked over to see Charlie on the floor. He'd wriggled out of his father's arms and had taken refuge in the small space under a seat. His father and Peggy were trying to coax him out, without much success.

"Just leave him," Billy said. "He'll come out in his own time. When he feels safe enough."

"And when the hell will that be?" his father snapped. "We'll only be safe when we get off this bloody train."

A true enough statement and one that brought a fresh round of hysterics from his son.

"For God's sake, watch what you're saying," hissed Billy. "Have you no idea what your son is going through? If it's bad for you, just imagine how much worse it must be for an 11 year old boy."

Suitably chastised, David dropped to the floor of the carriage and sat by the seat his son was under. He grabbed Charlie's hand and clasped it in his own. Neither spoke.

Satisfied that Charlie was alright, for now at least, Billy turned to look at the other passengers. Emma appeared calm, but was as pale as someone who hadn't seen the sun for many months, not just the two days they'd been held captive.

"He didn't shoot him," she mumbled. Billy had to strain to hear her. "Kourash didn't shoot him. I knew he wouldn't."

The idea seemed to comfort her and she smiled at Billy, who personally didn't think there was anything to bloody smile about.

Hazel was rocking and keening, her hands wrapped protectively around her bump. Billy hoped to God all these shocks didn't bring on an early labour.

But it was Colin that was the problem, Billy realised.

The man's pallor was as grey as his business suit. He was still sweating profusely and was now grabbing at his arm, as if he was trying to keep hold of a limb that refused to obey his brain's instructions. Billy bent down by Colin's seat and reached to undo the tie that Colin had insisted he kept on. More than likely his one grip on reality, in a situation as alien as a Hollywood disaster movie.

"Here, let me help," Billy said as he removed the tie and undid the top few buttons of Colin's pin-striped shirt.

"Emma, get Colin some water."

No reaction. She was staring at Kourash. Her face wore a beatific expression, like a believer staring at a picture of Christ.

"Emma," he called harshly, "get Colin some bloody water!"

She responded as if coming out of a trance. "What?"

"Water for Colin. I'm really worried about him. I'm afraid he might have a heart attack."

"Oh, sorry, yes, of course," and she proceeded to do as Billy asked, her eyes coming back into focus.

Billy left Colin's side to go and berate Kourash for his actions, but didn't get a chance, as the hijackers turned on their leader, gibbering and gesticulating. Billy couldn't understand what they were saying, but saw the sneer on Kourash's face. He doesn't care what they think, Billy realised, as Kourash majestically tossed his head and looked around the carriage with distain. This is his show and we're all just along for the ride. Hijackers and hostages alike.

Needing to contact Crane, Billy casually stood up and slipped, un-noticed, into the toilet.

10:15 hours

"What in Allah's name do you think you are doing?"

"This was supposed to be a peaceful protest."

"This is the second time you've fired the gun."

"There was to be no shooting."

Kourash held up his hands, signalling for silence.

"Don't be so stupid," he said. He realised that his fellow hijackers hadn't a clue what needed to be done. And would be done. "The oppressors need to fear and respect us if we want them to agree to, and act upon, our demands," he continued. "Otherwise we're just sitting ducks. A target for anyone who wants to take a pot shot at us."

"Well," said one, appearing to be slightly braver than the others, "let's hope that's the end of it."

"No my comrades," said Kourash, "it's just the beginning. Now go and do your jobs. Two of you go to the other carriage as lookouts and the rest of you stay here and keep your eyes on the hostages."

As the hijackers scuttled to do Kourash's bidding, Emma stood and asked, "How could you do that to Mick? He's a fellow human being. What is wrong with you?"

By way of a reply he grabbed her arm and dragged her into the cab, the staring eyes of the remaining hijackers following them.

Once he had closed the door he asked, "Do you have a family, Emma?"

"No, not really," she replied. "My mother died in childbirth and my father brought me up until he died in a car accident when I was 11." She sat down in the driver's seat, the springs creaking in protest.

"So you were orphaned and abandoned?"

"I suppose so, if you want to put it that way. Why do you want to know? What difference does it make?"

"Because I was orphaned and abandoned also," Kourash said.

"But I thought you came to live in England with your uncle and aunt, who became your surrogate parents."

"Oh yes, I did, but my real parents discarded me. Pushed me away. Didn't want me. I've resented them for doing that all my life."

Kourash turned around and leaned against the instrument panel, looking directly at her.

Emma was silent for a moment then said, "I suppose you could look at it like that. But you could also say that your parents made the ultimate sacrifice to give you a better start in life than you would have had in Afghanistan."

"But Afghanistan is my home, my life, my destiny. Not England. And they took that away from me. Took my homeland away," Kourash felt himself becoming emotional, so turned that sorrow into anger. "So now I'm fighting for it."

"To show how dedicated you are, I suppose?" asked Emma.

"Yes, that's it. What about you, don't you feel abandoned by your parents?"

"Of course, but it wasn't their fault. They didn't mean to."

"Aren't you lonely and alone, though?" Kourash desperately wanted this calm, serene young woman to feel as he did.

"Yes, of course," she said slowly. "But I'm trying to make the best of my life without them. Trying to make them proud of me."

"See, I knew it! That's the same as me. I'm trying to make my parents notice me. To make them proud of me. Proud of the way I am standing up for Afghanistan. And to make the Afghan people proud of me as well. When this is all over, Emma, will you tell them? Tell the world that I did what I did for my country? Tell them how I feel about Afghanistan?"

"Why? Why should I tell anyone that? Divulge our conversations?" she looked at him confused yet again by this charismatic young man.

"Because I want to be taken seriously. To be held in some esteem. For people to understand me and understand my actions."

When he took her hand, stood her up and enfolded her in his arms, she didn't resist and leaned into him.

"Very well," she whispered. "I'll tell them for you."

10:20 hours

K didn't shoot Mick. Everyone okay for now. K v volatile and unstable. One wrong move could tip him over the edge.

Crane had just relayed Billy's text message to the team. Even though Mick hadn't been shot, it didn't make them feel any easier. Everyone was on edge from too much caffeine and too little sleep. As he sat around the table looking at the others, Crane had a sudden urge to get away. Scraping back his chair he left the confines of the station building and walked up and down the platform, turning his lighter over and over in his pocket as he did so. He was even past the need for nicotine, which was only serving to make him jumpy every time he smoked a cigarette, which was far too often.

In the distance he could see the cannon-like telescopic lenses of the news photographers and television crews who were keeping the train under constant observation. For most of the unseen newspaper readers and television watchers around the world, the media offered a tiny glimpse of yet another 'terrorist drama'. But would any of them dwell on the underlying causes of such violence? Would anyone think of the hostages involved in the tragedy? Think about what it must be doing to their tattered nerves and slim resources?

All the viewers saw was a kaleidoscope of images running past their eyes every day. Images which only scratched the surface of the incident and didn't reflect the price the hostages must be paying. Billy was trained, young and strong. But Crane knew the civilians wouldn't be able to cope as well as Billy. The hostages may well come out of the incident with their lives, but those lives would never be the same again. Fair enough some would emerge stronger, but others would be broken in both mind and spirit. The hijackers may imagine they're involved in a Holy war, but what right did they have to wage war against innocents? Crane didn't know. He could only pray that it would come to a bloodless end. And soon.

Ever since the gunshot had rolled around the idyllic Yorkshire Dales like a harbinger of death, there had been intense anticipation in the press paddock. Reporters gabbled into recorders and mobile phones. Presenters checked their appearance for a live television report. At last, something was happening. Eyes shone, lips were licked and glossed, hair flicked and ties straightened. Harry Poole and Diane were no different to their colleagues in their immediate reaction. At last some real news. Something to report. But then, for them, a different kind of reality set in.

"Oh my God, do you think Billy's alright?" Diane hissed to Harry.

"Diane, we've no bloody idea what's going on."

"But..."

"So don't worry over what you can't control and concentrate on what you can," he said. "We've a job to do, just like everyone else here. Let's keep our minds concentrated on the here and now, not on what might have happened." Harry was buffeted and pulled about by people as he tried to stay close to Diane. "For God's sake!" he shouted at someone who had just cannoned into him, but the man disappeared into the melee without apology.

"Come on," said Diane. "Let's find out what's going on. It looks like a spokesman is going to make an announcement," and they followed the rest of the herd to the Information Point.

The hapless spokesman was inundated with questions. Members of the media were all shouting at once. All demanding answers. All wondering what the hell had just happened. When no suitable response was given, the press conference turned into a free for all. Questions peppering the spokesman like buckshot.

"Have the hijackers all been identified yet?"

"What about the hostages?"

"When are you going to give us background information on them?"

"Who are the hijackers?"

"Where are they from?"

"Please, quiet, please," the man begged. Then someone handed him a piece of paper. Harry smiled as the look on the spokesman's face suggested that the scrap of paper was his salvation.

Clearing his throat the spokesman shouted into the microphone and waved the paper around like a trophy he'd just won, or as if he was giving a thank-you speech at the Oscars. "There will be a full press conference in one hour. At that time we will share any appropriate information with you on the current situation regarding the hostages and the hijackers."

But as he began to thank them for their patience, he was talking to himself. As quickly as they'd arrived, the press retreated, like a wave that had crashed on the shore and expelled its energy. They were all being sucked back, anxious to return to their equipment. Protective of their prime broadcasting spots, from where they beamed their television reports across the world.

11:00 hours

"Keane. I want the prisoners released. In two hours." Kourash spoke to Keane as though addressing a child.

Kourash waited a beat for Keane's reply. Two beats. Three beats. But none came.

"Very well. I take it that's your answer. In that case, start releasing prisoners in two hours, or I'll blow up the train."

"Kourash, listen…"

"No, Keane, I've listened to you long enough. Threatening to kill hostages isn't working. It isn't making any difference. So now I will blow up the train."

"Kourash, please, we're trying. Diplomats are working night and day…"

A harsh laugh escaped from Kourash's throat. Pushed out of his mouth by the force of his anger.

"Stop giving me that bullshit! Release prisoners and I'll release hostages. Do nothing and I'll blow up the train. Your choice."

Kourash realised there was no point in continuing the conversation, so he replaced the receiver. He looked out of the cab window and imagined the eyes of the world on the little train. Did anyone understand what was really happening here? Understand what he was trying to do?

He hoped so. But thought not.

He wondered about Keane. What did he look like? What sort of man was he? Did he have family? Brothers? Sisters? Had he ever had an injustice done against his family? Was there a spark of understanding in him for Kourash's cause?

He hoped so. But thought not.

And what of the hostages? He was trying to be understanding of their fear and anger. He knew they hated him for what they perceived he was doing to them. Taking their liberty. Frightening them half to death. Forcing them to stay on the train against their will. He'd told them why he was doing it. To get his brothers released from prison. From where they'd been held for months, even years, without being charged. Without being tried. Without any justice. Did they understand him at all?

He hoped so. But thought not.

He closed his eyes in prayer, willing Allah to give him the strength and determination to carry out his threats. For he must show no weakness. He also prayed that it would be over soon.

"Blow up the train, Keane? Did I hear correctly?" the Colonel asked.

Keane nodded his agreement, for a moment unable to find any words. Unable to shake the fear and responsibility he was wearing like a hair shirt. If Kourash did blow up the train it would be... would be... All His Fault.

"How likely is he to carry out his threat?" Crane pulled Keane's attention away from his well of self-pity.

"How likely?"

"Yes, Keane. Come on, you're the bloody psychiatrist, or psychologist, or whatever the hell you call yourself. Whatever it is, you study the human mind and human behaviour. What is Kourash most likely to do?"

Keane took a deep breath. Decision time. "Honestly?" he stalled.

"Keane," Crane growled, a low rumbling warning.

"Very well. I think it's unlikely he will go that far." Now he'd started to speak Keane felt better. Hiding behind his professional judgement, he was able to detach himself from the horror that was the reality of what was happening.

"On what do you base that opinion?" the civil servant, Hardwick, who never said much asked.

"His previous behaviour. Not shooting to kill Potts." In response to Crane's glare he quickly continued, "I know Potts died, but I don't think Kourash intended a kill shot, more of a warning shot."

"Anything else?"

"Yes, the fact that he didn't kill the train driver, Mick."

"But we're not supposed to know that. We are meant to believe he did kill him."

"I know. And that's how we can call his bluff. We know he couldn't go through with actually killing a hostage, so the odds are that he won't be able to find the guts to blow up the train, after all." Keane was warming to his theories now, feeling more confident. "Kourash believes that we believe that Mick is dead. Our trump card is the fact we know he isn't. Therefore, we can surmise he's more likely not to blow up the train." There. He'd done it. Made the prediction.

"How would he blow it up anyway?" the Colonel wanted to know.

"That's the other thing that makes me believe Kourash won't carry out his threat. I don't think he can. We've no evidence that he has explosives or bombs on board."

"No, you're probably right," Crane was scratching at his cheek again. "Billy hasn't seen anything like that. And I don't see how they could have got a bomb onto the train." Crane indicated the still photographs on the boards. "From the CCTV footage showing them getting on the train, they've only got a couple of rucksacks between them."

"So we do nothing," said the Colonel.

"To be brutally honest, gentlemen," the normally reticent civil servant said, "President Karzia will not be going on television and he will not be releasing any prisoners. So it's a moot point really. Your job, Keane, is to stop Kourash doing anything like that, through negotiation."

"But I've nothing to negotiate with!" Keane had had enough. His anger got the better of him. "No one is giving me anything to work with," he shouted. All earlier warm feelings chased away by the storm clouds of his anger. "There are no concessions the Government are willing to make. All I can offer is food and water and bloody religious leaders. What am I supposed to say? Be a good boy Kourash and I'll send you up a cup of coffee. How do you take it? One sugar or two?"

As Keane slammed out of the station building, needing to get away, he wondered if any of them had heard his parting shot of, "Tossers."

11:15 hours

Everyone was beyond jittery. They didn't know what Kourash planned to do next, but could feel the tension emanating from him and from his fellow hijackers. Kourash had returned to the carriage and he and his men were having a huddled conversation. Not that they needed to whisper, none of the hostages could understood what was being said.

Billy didn't know what to do to make things better for the hostages. The temperature was rising in the carriage again, as the sun rose above the Yorkshire Dales and blasted its mocking rays onto the roof of the train. Being unable to open the windows made the fetid air hotter. They had plenty of water and unlimited access to it, so the problem for most of them, with the exception of Colin, wasn't physical. They weren't suffering from illness or hunger, or thirst, but simply from mental strain. From being cooped up. Unable to leave. Being held against their will. It was pure torture.

Billy's nerves were taut from watching the hijackers. From trying to work out what they would do next. From hoping his mobile phone battery would hold out so he could continue to pass information to Crane. All this procrastination was driving him mad. He decided to stop speculating and take a chance. He'd just ask.

"Kourash," he called, as the men finished their hurried discussion.

"Yes?" the word was a sneer and accompanied by a flash of anger in Kourash's eyes.

Jesus, thought Billy, he is wound up. Carefully he began, "We were just wondering if you could tell us what's going on? Where you are in the negotiations?"

"That is no concern of yours."

"Oh, come on, Kourash," Billy stood, not wanting to continue the conversation from his disadvantaged sitting position. "Have a heart. Tell us what's going on."

"Very well. Your so called Government, haven't acceded to my demands. So I've notched up my threat. If no prisoners are released from Bagram Detention Centre in the next two hours, then I'll blow up the train."

Kourash turned on his heel and stalked back into the driver's cab.

"Kourash!" Billy shouted. "Come back here! For God's sake man, you can't do that!"

But he was talking to the door that Kourash had closed behind him.

Billy realised he'd blown it. Perhaps it would have been better not to know what was going on after all. All he'd succeeded in doing was upsetting everyone further.

"Billy," whispered Hazel, "do you think he means it?"

"Who knows, Hazel? Personally I think he's playing mind games," Billy lied. "After all, we've not seen any bombs, have we? Not seen any explosives lying around."

"I wouldn't know what explosives look like, but that

doesn't mean there aren't any. Anyway, how do you know about explosives?"

Billy glanced at their captors, who for the moment seemed to be more interested in talking amongst themselves than listening to the hostages. But Billy still needed to be careful. Although they'd not heard them speaking English, it didn't mean they couldn't understand it. It could just be a ploy to put the hostages at ease and be able to eavesdrop on their conversations.

As Charlie was crying again and David and Peggy were comforting him, Billy hoped their noise would mask his conversation. He moved over to sit next to Hazel and indicated Mick should lean in to hear. "I'm not a personal trainer. I'm military."

That drew a gasp from Hazel and a grin from Mick.

"I'm managing to communicate with my boss via my mobile phone that I've stashed in the toilet. I'm feeding him information."

"Do you think they'll mount a rescue operation?" Mick's eyes were gleaming with anticipation.

"I think it's inevitable. But I don't know when it will be, or how they'll manage it. I just know that we have to be ready for when it does happen."

Hazel smiled as she rubbed her child-swollen belly. "It looks like I'll get a chance to meet you after all," she whispered to her unborn child.

"Don't tell anyone else, will you?" Billy asked them both. "We have to be careful. We don't want the hijackers to know."

"No worries, Billy," said Mick. "It's just like The Great Escape. Let's see how long we can fool them," and he got out of his seat and casually went to sit beside Peggy.

Billy didn't want to remind Mick of the reality that

many of the escapees from The Great Escape hadn't actually made it. Most of them had been killed by the Germans. Best to let him enjoy the stress-free moment, Billy decided.

"Who've you got waiting at home for you, Hazel?" Billy asked.

"My husband, mum and dad, a brother and a sister," Hazel smiled at the memory of them. "We're a very close knit family. In fact, I'm on my way back from seeing my sister in Carlisle. We went shopping for baby things the day before all this happened. It was all so normal. I can't begin to understand how or why this has happened."

"Do you work?" Billy continued, wanting to turn her thoughts away from the situation on the train.

"Mmm, nothing fancy, just behind the till in my local supermarket. Well, I did. I'm on maternity leave."

"Will you go back to work after the baby's born?"

"I was planning to, but now I'm not so sure. Maybe my baby is more important than money, don't you think?"

"I think that whatever you decide to do, will be the right thing for you and your family."

"What about you?" Hazel asked Billy. "Have you anyone waiting for you?"

"I'd just been to visit my mum and dad. They live in Carlisle."

"And is there anyone special waiting for you?" Hazel teased.

"Well my boss is. He's pretty special."

"Idiot," she laughed. "You know what I mean."

"I know," Billy looked down. "Maybe. I'm not sure yet..."

"Go on."

"I did meet someone I wasn't expecting to, last weekend. We had a pretty good time," Billy turned his head and smiled at Hazel. "But she's not exactly a suitable choice of girlfriend."

"Now I'm intrigued. You can't stop now. Why on earth isn't she suitable?"

"She's a reporter for the local paper. Always asking questions. Always probing. Wanting a quote on this that or the other." Billy dropped his head again. "But the other night we had a pact. No talk of work from either of us."

"And did it work?"

"Yes, it worked."

"So you'll see her again?"

"I hope so. I was planning to see her on Friday, before all this happened," Billy admitted. Not just to Hazel, but to himself.

As he left Hazel to get a drink of water, he looked at the blackened windows, as if to see beyond the obstruction, to the media and families waiting some distance away. Wondering if Diane knew he was on the train? Wondering if she cared? Wondering if she was out there waiting for him?

11:30 hours

As promised, at the next news conference, the press were handed out details of not just the hijackers, but also the hostages. Harry and Diane scanned the list and the scant information it contained.

"Looks like that's your green light, Diane," said Harry. "Pull together everything you've got on the hostages and hijackers, write two articles and I'll look them over."

Diane's eyes shone in anticipation of the praise to come from Harry when he realised how good her writing was and how effective her investigations. She'd managed to get a fair bit on the hijackers, but not the hostages, so her plan was to phone any contacts she had in the various locations pertaining to the hostages and get them to dig up whatever they could. In the meantime she would write the first piece on the hijackers. She turned away from Harry, leaving him to catch the remainder of the news conference, eager to get on with the job in hand. She had a lot of favours to ask and just had to hope that in the future everyone wouldn't call them in all at once. Or sell her out again.

As she walked she read over the details they'd been

given on the hijackers, wondering how well educated, normal young men, of good standing in their community, could turn out to have been radicalised. One of the men on this list had to be the leader. The one who had turned the others. More than likely that Kourash bloke. The one who's relatives had done the interview. That was the angle for her article, she decided. Pure speculation, of course, but then again that was fast becoming her trade mark.

Her attention was drawn away from the piece of paper in her hand by a noise overhead. The whoomp whoomp of rotary blades from a fast approaching helicopter, mesmerised the ladies and gentlemen of the press, as it swooped low overhead. Then, with a collective roar, everyone raced back to their stations, craning their necks to watch the spectacle in the sky as they ran. Diane realised that they were all hoping to God their cameramen and photographers had reacted quickly enough and were already filming. Harry's paper had a photographer on site and she raced towards him, the planning of her articles cast aside in favour of a new, more exciting development.

"What the fuck?" was Crane's reaction to the noise overhead as he chased Booth and Hardwick outside, just in time to see a small black helicopter pass overhead. There were no marking on it depicting the police, air ambulance or rescue, so Crane had to deduce that it was some idiot from the press, determined to be the one to get close up pictures of the train and the hostages.

"Keane!" Crane shouted as he ran back inside the station, "Tell Kourash..." but the remainder of his words were cut off by the ringing of the telephone.

Crane slid to a halt beside Dudley-Jones and listened as Keane tried to placate the hijacker.

"Kourash, this has nothing to do with us. It's not a military helicopter."

"You fucking bastards," was Kourash's reply. "I warned you. I told you to stay away. I told you what would happen if you didn't."

"Please listen. I don't know who they are. I repeat, this is not a police or military helicopter."

But Kourash wasn't about to be placated and continued screaming at Keane.

"Get them away from the train now Keane!"

"I can't. I don't know who they are," Keane was still speaking in his calm measured voice and Crane once again had to admire the man's restraint.

Crane looked at the overhead monitor, showing the live pictures from Sky News of the helicopter passing over the train.

"What are you doing about this," he hissed to Dudley-Jones. "For God's sake get that bloody helicopter away from the train."

"The local RAF station is scrambling, but it's going to take them about five minutes to reach us, sir."

"Christ alive, that's too long, anything could happen in five minutes."

Over the speakers, Keane was still trying his best to placate Kourash who, Crane could see on the television, was leaning out of the window of the driver's cab. In his fear and anger it seemed Kourash had forgotten about staying obscured from the authorities and the press. Remaining secure behind the darkened barriers he had created. But from the distance of the media field, even with their latest technology, Kourash was still as small as a stick figure in a Lowry painting.

"Do we know who the helicopter belongs to?" Crane demanded.

"Not at the moment, sir. The team have contacted the major news stations, who have all denied that it's one of their reporters," replied Dudley-Jones.

Crane had to assume the television stations were telling the truth, otherwise one of them would be beaming live close up shots of Kourash hanging out of the driver's cab. Crane peered more closely and Kourash seemed to be waving his fist at the machine. Was it a fist? With a chill Crane realised it wasn't just an arm Kourash was brandishing, but clasped in his hand was a machine gun.

Crane grabbed a piece of paper, scribbled something on it and rushed into the small room Keane was in. Even though Keane's voice had been calm, almost serene, over the speakers, Crane saw the extent of his anguish portrayed in his body movements. Keane was pacing and turning in the small room. He paced and turned several times before he noticed Crane.

As Keane looked up, Crane thrust the paper into the man's hand. Keane looked down and read the message: *Kourash is threatening the chopper with a machine gun*, just as a volley of bullets could be heard simultaneously out of the telephone handset and through the open window.

It had been bad enough when they'd heard the helicopter, but when the shooting started, that's when everyone really did fall apart. For Emma the world became a series of disjointed images. Charlie howling, holding out his arms to his father. Billy angry, looking up at the ceiling of the train, tracking the movements of the helicopter with his head. Hazel's arms wound protectively around her bump. Colin's grey face. His eyes closed. Lips moving. Praying, no doubt. She felt Peggy's arms snake around her shoulders, trying to comfort her. But all she felt was stifled.

Shaking off the woman's embrace, Emma looked towards the closed door of the driver's cab and screamed, "Kourash! No!"

Pushing her way through the men guarding the door, who seemed as stunned as everyone else in the carriage, she grasped the door handle and turned it. She pulled the door open as another hail of bullets wrenched through the air. Deafened and disoriented, Emma lurched through the opening. She fell against Kourash and grabbed hold of him, her knees buckling, her falling body dragging him back through the window.

He was mouthing something that she lip read as, "Bastards!" A sentiment she agreed with whole heartedly.

She once again called, "Kourash! No! Please!"

The fight seemed to go out of him at her words and he looked down at her, the anger clearing from his eyes. He put his weapon down on the floor, as the noise of the helicopter receded into the distance and then replaced the telephone handset, cutting off Keane's voice that was still babbling on, unheeded.

"What's the matter, Emma?" he grinned at her. "Surely you don't think I was trying to hit the helicopter?"

His mercurial change of mood confused her. Of course she thought he'd been trying to shoot down the helicopter. Everyone must have thought the same thing. She heard jabbering behind her and turned to see the other hijackers crowded around the door, pushing and shoving for a better view, but unwilling to enter the cab. It seemed the hijackers were as afraid of their leader as the hostages were.

"I was only scaring them off. Keane told me it was nothing to do with the authorities, so I guessed it was someone from the press wanting to get close up pictures. So I thought I'd give them something to write about, that's all. Shake them up a bit. Give them interesting pictures that they can flash around the world. I don't want the news story going stale, do I?"

But Emma wasn't at all sure that was what he was trying to do. She needed reassurance. As if reading her thoughts, he reached out, helped her off the floor and kissed her forehead.

13:00 hours

The minutes had crawled their way into hours in the waiting room and the hands of the clock on the railway station wall had finally reached the latest deadline for releasing prisoners. The dapper civil servant wasn't looking quite so dapper anymore, as Hardwick disconnected the call he had been on. The Prime Minister had just closed the COBRA meeting. The edict was clear and concise. There was to be no giving in to Kourash's demands. A unanimous decision.

Even though he knew it was coming, the verdict still felt like a hammer blow to Crane. He wondered what the decision would have been if any of the Cabinet had a relative on the train? The Prime Minister even? Would it have made any difference? Could that have swayed the decision? Personally Crane would have fought for some leeway if he'd had the opportunity of addressing the meeting. Pie in the sky, he knew. But God damn it, Billy was on that bloody train and as far as Crane was concerned, he was family. Just as much as Tina and his son were family.

Crane had spoken to Padre Symmonds earlier in the day. Trying to get some perspective on the whole thing, he supposed. Certain that he could talk to the Padre in complete confidence, he'd outlined what was happening and shared with him the secret of Billy's involvement. Captain Symmonds had worked with Crane and Billy often enough to understand the two of them. He understood and respected Crane's frustration as he railed against the hijackers, the people in command and even God himself.

The Padre had finished the conversation by saying that he would pray for everyone involved and particularly for a speedy end to the disaster that was unfolding on everyone's television set, car radio, newspaper and internet news pages.

All Crane could do was to caution the Padre when it came to praying for them all. "Be careful what you pray for," he'd said. "For you have to live with the consequences of those prayers. Whatever happens, people are going to die."

It was now time to see what the outcome would be, when Kourash realised there was to be no release of prisoners and that Bagram Detention Centre was staying open.

"What do the latest drone pictures show?" Colonel Booth asked Dudley-Jones.

"No change, sir. One driver's cab and one carriage empty. The other two occupied. Everyone seems to be crowded into those."

"So the strategy seems to be get everyone together and blow them all to kingdom come," Crane said, unable to keep the bitterness out of his voice. "How can the Prime Minister effectively sign the death warrant of a group of innocent hostages?"

"It's for the greater good," the civil servant Hardwick snapped, not so civil anymore. "There's no point debating it. We can't change the decision."

"That's all very well, but it's not your friend who's on the train," Crane slammed his fist into the table in his frustration.

"We don't know for certain that Kourash does have explosives on board, sir," Dudley-Jones said as he pulled his headset off and massaged his ears.

"I suspect that's a vain hope, but thanks anyway." Crane acknowledged the young man's attempt to pacify him.

Turning to Keane he asked, "Do you know what you're going to say to Kourash? It seems to me that this time you're not going to be able to dissuade him from carrying out his threat."

As Keane opened his mouth to reply, the phone rang. Jumping off the desk he'd been sitting on, Keane took the few paces to the telephone in the shop. Crane watched Keane hesitate before grasping the handset and raising it to his ear.

"Hello, Kourash," Keane said, in that calm and untroubled tone that Crane was in awe of.

"So, I take it you are ready to watch your people die?" Kourash's whisper was more deadly than a shout and the venom behind those few words conjured up an image of a King Cobra, coiled and ready to strike. Its flared hood and piercing intelligent eyes a perfect piece of imagery to describe Kourash, Crane decided. He looked at the picture they had of the hijacker. His haughty, puffed up visage sneering down at Crane from his elevated position on the incident board.

"Please, Kourash, there's no need to kill anyone. I'm still working with the authorities to try and meet your demands. I'm sure I can get some concessions for you."

"Well, I'm not sure, Keane. In fact I think your

efforts could be described as pathetic. As far as I'm concerned you're a failed negotiator. Remember what I told you before. Any deaths are a stain on your hands. Every time you look at them, you'll see their innocent blood, spilled because you couldn't save them."

"Kourash…"

"Goodbye, Keane."

As the line went dead, Keane replaced the telephone receiver and held his hands up in front of his face. Staring at them in horror, as though they were already covered in the blood of the innocents. As the sound of the explosion reached Ribblehead Station, Keane buried his head in his tainted hands. And Crane fell into the nearest chair.

13:05 hours

To be fair, Kourash had the decency to warn them of the explosion. Warn them that he was going to blow up the empty carriage at the end of the train. But it hadn't helped. It was yet another body blow to the already damaged armour the hostages were desperately trying to protect themselves with. Colin fainted as the shock waves pulsed through the train carriage. Flying shrapnel tattooed the darkened windows, making everyone jump and Charlie screamed and screamed in terror. Billy and Mick rushed to Colin's side and poured water over his face to revive him. Colin wasn't best pleased and as he surfaced, spluttering and swearing, he pushed away Mick's hand, as he attempted to get up off the floor.

Billy looked around at his forlorn band of desperates and felt useless. There hadn't been any chance to try and overpower one of the hijackers and grab his gun. They were always in two's, never alone and very protective of their weapons. Billy had come to the reluctant conclusion that he wasn't going to be able to mount a single handed rescue of the hostages. Not without getting any of them killed. And he couldn't take that chance. It wasn't fair on them. Now, if he'd been with a couple of mates, well that would have been different. But as it was he had to push away his military frustrations and concentrate on trying to keep everyone alive.

And that was looking more and more dodgy. Colin didn't look as though he would last more than a couple of hours. Death was already circling around him. Billy could almost see the dark shadow of the angel of death flittering across Colin's face. The latest shock had been a close one. It didn't seem that Colin's heart could take very many more shocks like that. And as for Hazel, all he needed was for her to go into labour. Peggy was alright, mostly taken up with caring for Charlie and his dad, David, who usually wore a bemused expression. His mind didn't appear to be with them most of the time. He looked very much out of his depth at having to spend so much time with his son. It seemed to Billy that his wife must have done most of the parenting. David was being presented with a perfect opportunity to bond with Charlie and help him through this terrible ordeal. Instead it seemed he was failing miserably as a father and a man.

Dismissing David, Billy turned to look at Mick, who was returning to his seat after helping Colin. Mick was one of those men who would give anything a go, but without much thought behind his actions. But he was a good man, trying his best in the most horrendous of circumstances, but way out of his depth. He was still concerned about the rail network and kept going on to Billy about the disruption to the railway system.

Next to Mick, Emma was curled into a ball in her seat. She was a strange one, mused Billy. Obviously intelligent, but not experienced in life, cocooned in her studies at university and no doubt equally cocooned by mummy and daddy, who naively thought they could protect their daughter by not exposing her to the harsh realities of life. Well she was getting a big dollop of reality now. Billy had thought, even hoped, she might lean on him to help her get through this, but it seemed she had become fascinated by Kourash. Okay the man was certainly dynamic and attractive in a dark smouldering way. The complete antithesis of Billy. Oh well, he couldn't win them all, he supposed, and anyway there was someone back in Aldershot who liked his open friendly face and fair-haired good looks. But he pushed away the creeping thoughts of Diane. He had to concentrate on the job in hand. He'd think about her later. He needed to make sure he survived this first. Otherwise he'd definitely never see her again.

Back to the job in hand. He had to get a message to Crane. The explosives were in the bicycles themselves. They'd obviously packed the frame full of sticks of something explosive and had set the bomb off using a mobile phone. That meant there may be explosives in all six bicycles. He had to hurry.

Crane had never felt so relieved to get a text. As the merry tune emanated from his phone, indicating a message, he shouted, "Yes!" as he pressed the button, but no one heard him, the other members of the team being more interested in shouting at each other.

"Where are the fucking pictures from the drone!" yelled the Colonel.

"Coming, sir, coming," gabbled Dudley-Jones as he frantically keyed in instructions to show the pictures on the large screen that everyone was watching.

"Come on, come on," mumbled Keane, who had come out to join them.

"How will we know if anyone is in the rubble?" asked Hardwick, wringing his hands and looking like Scrooge on a bad day.

"The thermal imaging camera on the drone will show up any bodies, as long as it gets there in time, while they're still warm. Isn't that right, Dudley-Jones?" Booth snapped at the poor intelligence operative, who was still clicking away and clearly trying not to panic.

As the smoke cleared and the live feed showed pictures of a big flat mangled mess where the rear carriage had been, Dudley-Jones switched to a thermal view.

As everyone edged closer to the screen for a better look, Crane shouted, "Everyone's okay! Kourash must have moved them out of danger!"

"Where? How? Is that what all these colours mean?" the civilian was pawing at the Colonel's uniform in his desperation.

"Stop going on about colours," said Crane. "Billy has just sent a message," and he went on to tell them about the explosives being in the bicycles and that the carriage had been empty of people.

"Thank God," breathed Keane as he perched on the edge of the table, the Colonel and Hardwick having taken the nearest chairs.

"Should we let Kourash know, that we know, that no one's hurt?" wondered Booth, looking at Keane, as sanity returned to the room.

But it was Crane who answered. "No way! He might realise we have inside information that could only come from someone on the train. No. I won't have it. It will put Billy at risk. Come on, sir. Please?" Crane was prepared to grovel to a superior officer if it got him what he wanted. But he wouldn't make a habit of it.

The Colonel looked away from the screen to be met by beseeching looks from Crane and Dudley-Jones.

As the telephone link to the train began to ring, Booth nodded his head in agreement. "Okay, Keane, pretend we don't know what's going on."

As Keane rushed to answer the phone, the Colonel looked Crane square in the face. "You do realise we have to block all mobile phone transmissions from the train now, don't you?"

Crane held Booth's stare. But realised he had to concede that now. He'd fought against that course of action for the past 24 hours. Not only to enable Billy to send and receive messages, but also so that the intelligence boys could monitor any phone calls the terrorists made.

"But," Crane stalled.

"No buts, Crane. The speech about monitoring phone calls won't work. Kourash hasn't made any. We've no choice. We can't risk Kourash setting off anymore bombs. I'm ordering the mobile phone signals to be blocked."

"Um, sir?" Dudley-Jones sounded uncertain and as Crane and the Colonel turned to look at him, his face was yet again beginning to flush with embarrassment.

"What?"

"I don't, um, think it will help."

"It won't help? Of course it will, without the mobile phone network Kourash can't blow up anymore bicycles."

"Yes he can, sir. I've just had word through. None of the mobile networks were used to trigger the explosion. Kourash must have a secure link, set up just for that purpose."

13:15 hours

Kourash replaced the telephone receiver, a look of pure joy on his face. He had done it. He was winning! He knew the authorities were taking him seriously now. He'd known violence was the only language these people understood. After all, he'd learned his lessons well at the Mosque and at the training ground. It irritated him that his fellow hijackers didn't share the same view. Had wanted everything to be low key. He laughed at their ignorance. No guns. No violence. No killing. That was their edict and it just wouldn't have worked. He needed to speak the international language of terrorism for anyone to take him seriously and that's precisely what he had done.

Although he hadn't got to the killing stage just yet. He hadn't told the stupid man who called himself a negotiator if he'd killed anyone in the explosion. Simply left it to Keane's imagination. Which he was sure would be working over-time now. He envisaged Keane as a dried up, wrinkled prune of a man, unable to make any decisions for himself. Pulled and jerked like a marionette by his masters in Government. The masters who had seriously under estimated Kourash.

The conversation he'd just had with Keane had underlined his victory. Keane had told him, in a broken voice, that he was sorry that nothing had happened to make Kourash's demands come true. But that he was sure the authorities would do everything they could now, to put pressure on President Karzi and ensure, at the very least, the release of his brother.

Not wanting to appear easily convinced, Kourash had put another deadline in place of two hours. In two hours he wanted, if nothing else, confirmation from the President personally that arrangements were being made to release some prisoners.

He wanted to share his victory with somebody. He fleetingly thought about his fellow comrades and immediately dismissed them. They were fast becoming nothing but pawns in his grand plan and the overtures of friendship he had made to them, were being exposed for what they were worth. Nothing. He had used them. Recruited them because he needed support. Made them feel they were vital elements in his plan, when in reality they weren't.

No, he would share this moment with Emma. She would understand. He had always been attracted to western women. Liked their independence, their forthrightness. Saw it as a challenge, he supposed, and idly wondered how long it would take him to break Emma. To make her fall so far under his spell that she would do his bidding without question and see him as her leader and her protector. He smiled at the thought of her subservience and enjoyed for a moment the sexual stirrings brought on by the vision. Yes, he would call for Emma. He was ready for her.

13:20 hours

After that fiasco, Crane knew they had no choice but to storm the train and do it as soon as possible. Various plans were being poured over by the Chiefs of Staff Committee and pitched to COBRA. Crane and the Colonel favoured the only plausible scheme to their mind. A night raid, or rather early morning raid. When the hijackers least expected it. In those early morning hours when the body really hadn't much of an option but to take the rest it needed. When sleep was deep, so anyone being rudely awakened by an attack would be disadvantaged, befuddled and disorientated. They would lose precious seconds before they reacted, as they tried to make sense of the chaos around them.

But at the end of the day it was the decision of those far more experienced than he was in such matters. Crane wasn't a strategist, an expert in mounting rescue missions. He was an expert in catching criminals and knew when to admit his limitations. While he was waiting for the decision to come down from COBRA, he wandered into Keane's small room, where he found him staring at the telephone, the lone instrument silent for the moment.

"You alright?" he asked what was clearly a stupid question. Keane looked haggard and harried, pushed and pulled between the two warring factions. Trying his best in the face of an impossible task. As an answer, Crane simply got thrown a look.

"Sorry, idiotic question I know. But really, Keane, why do you do this? How can you take the strain?"

Keane smiled weakly at Crane. "I must admit that every time I do this, I end up losing a little more of myself. It's guilt, I suppose. Why I keep doing it."

"Guilt? What the hell do you have to be guilty about?"

Keane got to his feet and went to stare out of the small window, his back to Crane. But he continued talking. "In my first job as a negotiator, I was full of myself. To the point of arrogance, really. I'd finished my degree, done my training with the police and was on the graduate fast track program. "Oh yes," Keane turned back to Crane, "I thought I was the dog's bollocks. No one could teach me anything. I was going to make a name for myself as some sort of stellar negotiator. The man who could talk anyone down."

"I guess you don't feel like that anymore?"

"No. Not since that first job."

"The first one?"

"Yep. A hostage situation. A man had barricaded himself into his house with his family, brandishing a shotgun threatening to kill his wife and two kids." Keane turned away from Crane again.

Crane decided to keep his mouth shut. If Keane wanted to confide in him, he would. He wouldn't need any prompting.

After taking a deep breath, Keane said, "I got the kids out. But not the wife. The bloke killed her and then himself. So I failed."

"But if you got the kids out, why do you think you failed?"

"Because I got their mother killed. After seeing the look on the children's faces, their anguish, their fear, as they were led away by a social worker. They'd gone from having two parents to being orphans in the blink of an eye. Pushed into a system that wouldn't care about them. That's why I feel guilty."

"Keane. It wasn't your fault. It was the man's fault. He was the one who pulled the trigger, not you."

"Then why does it feel like I did?"

Crane didn't know what to say to that and was glad of the call from the Colonel, telling them to get back in the room on the double.

The Colonel drew himself up to his full height and said, "The Prime Minister has made a decision, based on the advice of the Chiefs of Staff Committee. There is to be a night raid on the train."

"When?" asked Crane.

"Tonight, if possible, but it depends on the weather. There's a cold front on the way, bringing with it wind and rain. The cloud cover will ensure no moonlight and the storm will dampen the sound of the lads going in. It's our best chance and the Prime Minister wants this over and done with as soon as possible."

Crane and Keane nodded in agreement.

"So I just keep on bluffing and blustering, then?" said Keane.

"Afraid so," Booth said. "I know you've got a bloody awful job and you're doing the best you can, Keane, but you'll never be able to talk him into letting the hostages go. You do know that?"

"Of course, sir. I understand that, basically, Kourash

hasn't any idea what he's doing. Any suggestion that he could take on the might of the British Government was nothing more than a childish dream. He can't be allowed to carry on like this, with the whole world watching his and our every move. Thinking we would accede to his demands is nothing more than a fantasy."

"And an idealistic young man with a deadly fantasy is an extremely dangerous one," chipped in Crane.

"Quite so," agreed Booth. "So our job now is to keep everything as calm as we can, until the inevitable. From the minute he pulled the emergency cord on that bloody train, Kourash left us no choice. That simple act signed his death warrant."

13:30 hours

Emma glanced up from her book as Billy re-entered the carriage from the toilet, where he seemed to go a lot. She vaguely wondered why, but then dismissed him, much preferring to think about Kourash. Using her literary analytical mind to dissect his character and relating it to 'In Cold Blood', she thought he had factions of both Smith and Hicock in his personality. He had the friendliness of Smith, together with the 'little boy lost' facet that was so endearing. On the other hand, he also had the 'strutting cock' attitude frequently shown by Smith during his incarceration. If Capote thought the two killers were difficult to understand, she wondered what he would have made of Kourash.

The constant bombardment from Smith to Capote in terms of phone calls and letters, begging for his support and intervention in his case, reminded Hazel of Kourash's demands. His need to see her on her own. His desire to explain himself. Wanting her to understand his cause and his request for her to tell it to the world if it all went wrong. Would she be able to do him justice, she wondered? It seemed obvious that he and his fellow hijackers felt passionate about their cause. Which rationally, on the surface at last, seemed a good one. There were indeed many prisoners in Bagram Detention Centre held without charge, just as in Guantanamo Bay, but it didn't necessarily compute that they were innocent. But what if they were? What if there were more detainees like Kourash's brother, all going through a living hell? She had only been on the train two days and was already beginning to get cabin fever. It was the lack of liberty that was doing it. To see the Dales spread out around them when she went to talk to Kourash, brought it home to her that she couldn't just open the door and walk out.

She wasn't particularly bored, being able to tune out her surroundings and work on her dissertation based on Capote's book. But it was beginning to get harder to do that. Shouting, shooting, crying, helicopters overhead, were all conspiring to make her fearful and disconcerted. It was difficult to retain her equilibrium under such conditions. She'd tried to bond with Peggy and Hazel, but both women were older than her and had that maternal instinct to mother everyone, particularly Charlie. Emma had none of those feelings, she was far too young for those. But she recognised it left her a little isolated.

She looked at the window she couldn't see the Dales through and saw Kourash's image projected onto the black paper. She wondered when he would next call for her. At least he was interested in her, wanted to talk to her and maybe wanted more... she'd just have to wait and see what happened on the 'maybe more' front. A frisson of electricity pulsed through her body at the thought.

14:00 hours

When Crane went out for a cigarette break, Dudley-Jones followed him.

"I didn't know you smoked, DJ" Crane said, expecting the young man to get out a packet of his own particular brand of death.

"I don't, sir, I just needed to get away. I'm being bombarded with information and at the moment my brain just can't take it all in."

Indeed the young man did look like he'd been used as a veritable punch bag. As Dudley-Jones took off his glasses to rub his eyes, Crane saw his eyes were rimmed with red, the whites bloodshot with tiny veins skittering all over them, the lids puffed and sore. He couldn't help feeling sorry for the lad.

"Have the engineers finished looking for any damage to the viaduct from video and aerial photographs?" Crane asked.

"Yes, sir. It's still intact. No damage that they can see. The rails are buckled, obviously, but there doesn't appear to be any cracks in the structure itself."

"Thank God for that."

"Yes, well, I don't think it could be easily broken. It

took four years and a third of the workforce to build the viaduct. The stones they used are each two cubic metres in size and the viaduct was built in blocks of six arches for strength and safety. Apparently, every sixth pier is a wider one which gives stability to the structure. So if we had lost or damaged an arch, we'd lose six, but no more. Not all 24."

"Well that's good news," said Crane, but Dudley-Jones only managed a weak smile in reply. "Come on, what's bothering you?" Crane asked.

"In general? Or in particular?"

"Either, I guess."

"Well, it's this social media stuff that's really bugging me at the moment. Facebook and Twitter posts are spreading information about the state of Bagram Detention Centre, which in itself is whipping up support for the hijackers. People are agreeing with their stand. Calling the detention centre a disgrace. Popping up all over the place are stories from families who have a relative incarcerated there, saying they are innocent. They've not done anything wrong. And of course that means the media are picking up juicy bits of information and spreading the word. There seems to be a competition at the moment between the television stations, as to who can get the most awful, gut wrenching story about an innocent detainee."

"Dear God," breathed Crane. "But what about the other side of the story? The hostages' families must be going through hell. Aren't they being interviewed as well?"

"Of course they are, but they're not as good a news story. People crying is losing its appeal and anyway, we're keeping them away from the media as much as possible. At the moment, the media want fire and brimstone and that's what the other side are giving them. All that screeching, ranting and raving. You know how it is. I'm afraid they are swaying the tide of public opinion in favour of the hijackers."

"So what can we do to stop it?" Crane's hand went up to his face to subconsciously scratch at his scar.

"We've got to find a way of changing the tide. Get more support for the #*releasethehostages* campaign. Find a good angle to feed into Twitter and Facebook. That's as good a place to start as any. All the major newspapers and television stations are monitoring Twitter very closely and putting pictures of live feeds into their programmes."

"Any ideas as to how we can do that?" Crane needed Dudley-Jones' knowledge. He was definitely out of his depth when it came to social media and needed some guidance.

"Well, I guess we need to get a media mogul on our side."

"A media mogul?"

"Yes, someone who owns newspapers and television stations, get them to concentrate the efforts of their reporters into a 'release the hostages' campaign."

Crane shook a cigarette out of his box and lit it. His actions automatic, as his thoughts were elsewhere.

"Thanks, DJ," he said. "You've been very helpful," and he wandered off along the station platform, a plan beginning to emerge, like a genie appearing out of the smoke from his cigarette. By the time the smoke dispersed, Crane had a plan. But would he have enough time to implement it, before the train was stormed? The only person who could answer that question at the moment was the Colonel so Crane made his way back to the waiting room.

Swapping the pure air of the Yorkshire Dales for the despondent fug in the station building, Crane walked through the door and over to Booth, who appeared to have gotten a second wind. A half-hour break for a quick sandwich and a shower, had clearly helped Booth's disposition, which Crane figured meant he had a better chance of pulling his scheme off.

"Can I have a word, please, sir?" Crane interrupted the Colonel's watching of the latest news bulletins.

"What? Oh, it's you, Crane, come on then, spit it out."

"Well, sir, I think I've a plan to help change public opinion and ensure the country is behind the idea of the forces going in and rescuing the hostages when they do."

"At the moment that doesn't seem likely. Even though an hour ago he was all gung-ho and go in as soon as possible, the Prime Minister, for once, is actually bothered about public opinion and has now advised the Chiefs of Staff Committee that he can't authorise a rescue mission at the moment. Looks like he's actually being bullied into taking into account what the people want, or at least think they want. For too long his reputation has been sullied by accusations of not understanding what real people's lives are like. So for some reason he's decided that this is the issue he can hang his hat on and become a 'man of the people' or some such gibberish. Even though privately he wants a rescue mission to be launched as soon as possible."

"Jesus Christ. Is the man a bloody idiot?"

"You might think so, but I couldn't possibly comment," the Colonel smiled as he quoted the famous line from the television series, House of Cards. "Anyway, anything you can do to help change his mind would be greatly appreciated."

"I've got a question, first, sir. Is it likely the lads will go in tonight?"

"Haven't you listened to what I've just said, Crane?"

"Yes I have, sir, I just want it clarified."

"Alright then, is this plain enough for you; there will be no rescue mission tonight. For one the Prime Minister won't authorise it and for two the weather isn't right. The rain showers and cloud cover that were forecast have seemingly been delayed over Iceland would you believe, as if the bloody country hasn't enough to answer for after that volcano fiasco. So, they're not expected now until tomorrow night. So if we are to go in, tomorrow night is a better bet."

"Thank you, sir, then this is what I propose."

14:30 hours

The sight of Colin lying across two seats, looking more and more like a dead body lying on a mortuary slab with each passing hour, was finally too much for Billy. Colin's shirt was sweat stained, his trousers filthy. His discarded tie lay forlornly on the floor under his seat. The bloke was a bit of an idiot Billy decided, always bleating on about his office, the sales calls he had to make and the meetings he had to attend. He was forever insisting that people were relying on him, his employees, fellow directors and the like. But he was still a human being after all. So Billy really needed Kourash to let Colin go. He'd like Hazel to be released as well, but decided it was best not to push his luck. One would do for now. But how to achieve it? Kourash was well and truly pissed off with Billy, to the point that Billy doubted Kourash would entertain any of his suggestions. So he needed an in. He looked around at Hazel knitting, Peggy playing cards with Charlie, David watching them, Mick dozing by the blackened window and Emma, her nose in her book as usual. Emma. She could be the key. So he sidled over to her and asked if she'd help persuade Kourash to let Colin go.

"Of course I'll try, but what makes you think I have any sway with Kourash?" Emma was doing a fair job of looking surprised, but Billy was after all Military Police and well versed in when people were swinging a line. He was convinced she was a damn sight closer to Kourash than she was admitting. But if that was the way she wanted it, he was happy to play along.

"Oh," he said lightly, "it's just that you're the only one who has managed to have conversations with him. I've noticed he calls for you from time to time."

"Well, that's only to discuss a book," Emma sniffed.

"Discuss a book?" That was a new one on Billy.

"Yes, Truman Capote's In Cold Blood."

Not being a text he was familiar with, Billy didn't see the irony, only the image the book title conjured up.

"Sounds a bit gruesome to me," he said.

"Not so much gruesome as factual, actually," Emma said. "You see, it's written by a famous American writer who wanted to change..."

"Thank you, Emma, but I'm not here for a lecture in literature. Now, let's go and see what we can do for Colin."

"Oh, all right," said Emma, placing her book face down, still open at the page she was reading and they made their way to their captors, to ask permission to speak to their leader.

A few minutes later and they were back in the carriage. Billy wasn't sure what to make of Kourash at all. He'd listened respectfully to Emma's request and indeed his eyes did seem to soften when he looked at her.

No such look for Billy, however. Kourash's eyes glinted suspiciously and Billy felt Kourash hadn't completely fallen for his 'personal trainer' routine. They were dismissed with a wave of his hand and a polite promise to think about it.

Sitting in the driver's seat, with his feet up on the control panel, Kourash pondered the request. On the one hand he wanted to look good in Emma's eyes and agree to release Colin. One more step in making her fall under his spell. Her support for his cause something he might need in the future. On the other, he didn't want to appear weak in front of the authorities. Just ringing up and telling them he was letting Colin go, didn't seem the sort of thing a terrorist would do.

With a sigh, he lifted the telephone receiver to call Keane. He couldn't seem weak. He'd have to find another way to appease Emma.

When Keane answered, Kourash immediately went on the offensive. "Has President Karzi agreed to talk to me, face to face, via satellite link? I need to know what's going on, Keane."

"Hello to you too, Kourash," Keane replied, just a hint of sarcasm in his voice.

Well Keane was going to have to stop that if they were going to get anywhere, Kourash decided. He'd had enough of people not taking him seriously.

"Now look here, Keane. I'm serious. I need confirmation that the President will speak to me about Bagram and about the prisoners he is prepared to release. Do you understand?"

"Of course I do. It's just that..."

"Just what? What's the matter?" Kourash tried hard to keep any hint of desperation out of his voice. So far he hadn't persuaded anyone to do anything. And now it looked like he couldn't even get to talk to President Karzi. What the hell did he have to do?

"The President would like you to release a hostage as a gesture of goodwill. So he knows that if he does something for you, you'll reciprocate," Keane said.

"But I have to do something first? Damn you. You and your bloody tit for tat. You do this for me and I'll do that for you. You scratch my back..."

Kourash was having a hard time keeping his anger under control. But deep down he'd always known that he would have to release somebody eventually. Determined to not give anything away, Kourash decided to use the ideal gift unwittingly given to him by Emma and Billy.

"Very well, I'll let one hostage go."

"Who?" Keane said, just that bit too quickly, which made Kourash smile.

"We have an ill passenger. Colin somebody or other," Kourash deliberately sounded dismissive, as though the man meant nothing to him.

"What's the matter with him?"

"Why?" Kourash immediately countered, determined to keep Keane on the wrong foot.

"So that we can be sure we have the right equipment and medication to administer to him as quickly as possible."

"Oh, right. Something to do with his heart. Anyway, now I've decided to let Colin go, the rest is up to you. Let me know how you intend to collect him. And you can't come along the rails. Not after what's happened before. Men who've tried to kill me. Elders who tried to persuade me to give up. No, this time you play by my rules. No vehicles and no men." Kourash's voice had been getting louder and louder with each sentence, until in the end he was screaming at Keane. "Understand?" and then he slammed down the receiver for good measure.

He smiled in satisfaction and went to get a fresh bottle of water while he waited for Keane to come up with a rescue plan.

15:00 hours

Keane loped back into the control room. "You heard that then?"

"Yes, well done, Keane," the civil servant was obviously deciding to be civil this afternoon and Crane smiled to himself.

"Well, I've done my bit, so it's up to you lot how you get him out," Keane said and crossed the room to get a fresh cup of coffee.

"Well, if we can't go down the tracks," Crane started.

"Then we'll have to come in overhead," the Colonel finished.

"Exactly. And I take it you have a rescue helicopter already on stand-by?"

"Of course, Crane, I do know how to do my bloody job you know," the Colonel bristled.

"Indeed, sir," Crane bobbed his head in acknowledgement. "Just make sure they go in on the far side of the train. We want to keep this out of the public eye as much as possible."

"Huump," was all the reply Crane got. The Colonel turned his back on Crane and reached for a phone.

Crane drew Keane to the side of the room. "What do you think?" he asked. "Can we trust Kourash to let a hostage go?"

"Honestly?"

"Yes," Crane replied impatiently.

"I've no bloody idea."

Keane fell onto a chair with the air of a man defeated by the job and by life in general. His head hung as though he couldn't bear the weight of it anymore.

"Kourash will do whatever he wants to do," Keane mumbled at the floor and to Crane. "We can only hope for the best."

"Well you don't look too full of hope."

"If the truth be known I've given up hoping, Crane," Keane said. "What's that song? Que Será Será, or something. Whatever will be, will be," and Keane ended the conversation by walking outside.

Left alone, Crane scratched at his beard. What was that bastard Kourash up to?

15:15 hours

By 15:15 hours, the beat of the rotary blades could be heard faintly in the distance and Kourash called for Billy to bring Colin through to the front of the train. Billy held Colin's blubbery, half-unconscious form upright as best he could, dragging and twisting him as he pulled the man along the aisle. The other hijackers watched in amusement, but didn't offer to help. When Mick got up to assist Billy, he was stopped by the muzzle of an automatic weapon. Billy lurched through into the driver's cab, tripping up and falling through the door, just as the helicopter arrived overhead. Scrambling up, he heaved Colin to his feet and propped him up against the wall, holding him in place with his hands.

"They're going to drop down a harness. Put him in it and they'll winch him up," Kourash said to Billy, distain for both hostages clear in his hooded eyes.

"Aren't they bringing down a man?"

"No, I won't let them. You'll have to do it on your own."

Billy looked from Kourash to Colin and wondered who was the more stupid of the two. Kourash's madness seemed to know no bounds and Colin had proven time and again that he didn't live in the real world. Thought his money would cushion his path through life. Well life had certainly thrown Colin a curved ball this time. The man's pasty face was becoming greyer by the minute. His right arm still clutched his left. Slimy sweat covered his face and his shirt was opaque with it. Billy wasn't at all sure Colin was going to make it. But he had to try to save him. He'd made enough fuss about getting Colin released.

The rumble of the winch could be heard over the blam blam blam of the rotary blades and hailed the arrival of the harness. With one hand holding up Colin, Billy reached through the open cab door. Fingers stretching and grasping in the turbulent air, reaching for a swinging, swaying rescue harness.

"Kourash," Billy called, risking turning his head to look at the hijacker. "You'll have to help me. Either take Colin, or grab the harness. I don't much care which."

Billy's words were snatched away by the beating rotary arms. The buffeting air puffed up his shirt and rocked his body, which was perilously perched in the doorway. Billy looked down and wished he hadn't. The ground seemed to fall away under his feet as he teetered on the edge of the 100' drop. Colin's weight shifted and began to slide diagonally across the wall towards Billy, his bulk pushing Billy further into the yawning gap. The man Billy was trying to help, suddenly becoming a weapon turned against him.

As a gust of air caught Billy on the chest and pushed him slightly back, he took his chance and let go of Colin, pushing backwards with his feet and letting the air pummel his body backwards into the safety of the cab. He tumbled over Colin's feet and landed ignominiously on his arse. As he struggled to his feet he caught sight of Kourash's sneer.

"If you want Colin rescued, then you'll have to help, you bastard," Billy spat. "If you grab the harness, I'll hold him up and we can buckle him in. Or do you want the watching crew to tell everyone how they saw you deliberately kill Colin by not assisting in his rescue. Because he'll certainly die if he doesn't get off this train and if you don't help me, he's liable to fall out of the carriage, 100' to his death."

Kourash took a moment, before moving to the door. Holding the grab handle above the door, he leaned out and grasped the harness, easily swinging it into the cab, holding it firm so Billy could manoeuvre Colin into it and snap shut the buckles which would hold him in place.

Colin's head lolled against his chest and he seemed to be unconscious now. There had been no reaction at all when Billy buckled him into the harness. Billy wondered how much longer Colin had left in this world. But at least he'd done his best to save him.

Okay," he shouted to Kourash and gave a thumbs up sign, in case he hadn't heard.

Kourash nodded his agreement, leaned out of the doorway and spun a finger around in the air to indicate the winch could be reeled in.

Colin was dragged backwards out of the doorway, looking every bit like a puppet dangling from a string as his feet lifted off the floor and he was jerked away. Billy moved to go back into the carriage but Kourash shouted to him, "Wait," as he turned away from the door and picked up a satellite phone. Pushing the connection button he said, "Well?" into the handset and listened closely to the answer.

He put the phone back on the console panel, shook his head slightly, picked up his AK47 and swung it so it was pointing at the rapidly disappearing Colin. He let off a burst of fire, paused and then repeated it. Twice.

As the helicopter banked steeply away from the train, dragging Colin behind it as though the man was a whippet following the hare, Billy yelled, "What the hell are you doing?" astounded at the cruelty of the man. For someone like Billy, who had decency deeply ingrained in his psyche, he couldn't fathom what on earth had caused Kourash to try and bring down the rescue helicopter, never mind try and shoot Colin.

"They lied," Kourash growled. "So someone had to pay," and he smashed the butt of his automatic weapon into Billy's stomach.

15:20 hours

Billy gaped at the sight of Colin still dangling from the rescue helicopter, when Kourash reached over, slammed the door shut and pulled the blind down again. Cutting off the image as surely as Colin's life had been cut off.

"What the fuck are you doing?" Billy screamed from the floor, where he had been thrown by Kourash. But he could barely hear Kourash's reply as his ear drums were still trying to recover from the barrage of automatic fire being discharged in such a small space. He wallowed in a dream like world, sounds weaving around him as though Kourash was speaking in slow motion. What he was saying Billy had no idea, but he was ranting like the lunatic he clearly was. Spittle flew from his mouth as he threw invective after invective around the small space.

As Billy's hearing cleared, so did his mind, rage boiling through his body, surging wave-like, pulsing through him with every beat of his heart. He clawed his way off the floor, his lungs trying and failing to replace the oxygen smashed from his body by Kourash. Despite that, Billy threw himself at the hijacker, crashing into his back and flinging him against the control panel. Kourash dropped his gun in surprise. But he recovered quickly, pushing himself off the control panel and back towards Billy. Billy was flung to the floor once again, but immediately moved to try and grab the machine gun that had skittered across the floor and landed up against the outside door. Billy's hand reached for the prize. He just managed to touch the hot metal of the barrel when Kourash stamped on Billy's fingers. Keeping them trapped under his boot, Kourash reached down and retrieved his weapon. Only then did he release Billy's hand.

Rolling around in pain, Billy cradled his injured hand against his body and looked up at the wild eyed, wild haired man above him.

"You fucking bastard," Billy screamed as he scrambled to his feet, ready for another attack on Kourash. But Billy was stopped by the machine gun pointed at his chest and stayed where he was.

"What the fuck did you do that for?" Billy said, knowing he had to try and calm down. Getting himself shot or killed wouldn't help the hostages much.

"What's going on?" he gasped.

"Your puppet masters tried to trick me," said Kourash. "They said I would be able to speak to President Karzia himself. So I could ask him to release prisoners from Bagram Detention Centre. But they lied. Karzia won't be speaking to me. At the moment he is on a diplomatic tour of Iran, speaking to the press with the leaders. They are all together. On live television. He's no intention of talking to me. Either that or he doesn't even know what's going on here."

"Kourash..." But Billy's words were cut off by a slap across the face.

"Shut up. Go back to the others. Leave me alone."

Billy's good hand bunched and he'd started to raise it, when common sense took over. He had to be sensible. Retaliation would only make things worse, so he had to push away his anger and loathing for the man and back down. Not something that came naturally to Billy. Outspoken and headstrong were phrases often cited by Crane and indeed one such escapade had lost him a stripe and nearly lost him his place in the SIB.

It was a hard lesson to learn. To stop being a hothead and step back and find another way around a problem. Maybe that was what he would learn from the hijacking. If he survived, that was.

Turning away from Kourash, Billy opened the cab door and walked back into the carriage. Everyone surged towards him, all speaking at once, all wanting to know what had happened.

"We heard the gun-fire. What's happened?" Mick plucked at Billy's shirt.

"Is Colin alright?" Hazel's staring eyes were large in her pale face.

"All this is really upsetting Charlie," Peggy deliberately looked at the other hijackers, but they wouldn't meet her defiant gaze.

"Who did he shoot at?" Emma stood and looked at Billy, her voice carrying over the heads of the others.

"No one," Billy replied. "Kourash didn't shoot at anyone. He just fired a few warning shots, that's all."

As everyone sank back in their seats, Billy looked across at Emma. Relief was clear on her face. But who was the relief for? Relief that Colin hadn't been killed? Or relief that Kourash hadn't tried to kill anyone?

Billy wasn't sure and could only hope he'd done the right thing by keeping the truth from her.

16:00 hours

Colin's rescue had been a fiasco. There was no getting away from it. They were dealing with a mad man. Although, personally, Crane had always believed that Kourash was mad. Would someone in their right mind hijack a train and expect to change the long standing policy? The British Government would not negotiate with terrorists. End of. Simple.

No one would forget the images on television of the rescue helicopter banking away from the train, flying the dying hostage to Leeds hospital. A route that unfortunately took it over the crowded media field, from where the bullet holes were clearly visible on the side of the helicopter. And if you missed seeing the holes, there was no avoiding the plume of black smoke pouring from the tail of the aircraft. Thank goodness the crew had managed to winch Colin into the aircraft before flying over the media field. The pictures were flashed around the world at warp speed thanks to the internet and 24 hour live television. If Kourash wanted world-wide infamy, he certainly had it now.

There was only one good thing to come out of it. COBRA had agreed to Crane's suggestion to manipulate public opinion. A suggestion that had morphed into Colonel Booth's and Hardwick's idea, of course. It wasn't too much of a surprise to Crane. He'd always known of the power of the government, the British Army et-al, to feed selective bits of information to the public. The pieces of news the establishment wanted them to have. Their ability to keep information from the public was legendary. He himself had been involved in bringing an army cover-up to light, spun after a soldier had killed a woman. It was only the second killing that had tipped the balance and meant Crane was able to expose the cordon of lies the establishment had bound the truth in.

Crane pulled his thoughts away from a previous case, back to the current problem. There was a certain amount of support for Kourash and his merry band of compatriots, from ISIS, Muslim extremists and other loony fringe collectives. Add to them the calls from the liberals wanting a peaceful negotiated settlement and you had Muslims and Christians all calling for the same thing, albeit from different angles and for different reasons. They were effectively tying the Prime Minister's hands. Forcing him to enter into protracted negotiations.

The news programmes and newspapers had been full of background stories on the hijackers as well as the hostages and it was hard to tell who was garnering more support. There were heart wrenching stories of the innocents on both sides. The innocents in Bagram Detention Centre being held with no material evidence against them and the innocents on the train. All human beings who had legions of friends and families praying for their safe return.

So the plan was to manipulate public opinion. Get

everyone calling for the brave lads of the British Army, specifically the legendary SAS, to storm the train and rescue the hostages. To achieve this the Prime Minister had to sway public opinion and get the people of Britain to realise that the real heroes here were the poor innocent captives on the train, not their captors. It was time to start a whispering campaign on social media. Play ISIS and the terrorists at their own game.

Members of the Cabinet were primed and ready to speak to their contacts in the media. Senior Government figures were scheduled to give interviews. David Dimbleby was being approached about a special edition of the programme, Question Time, with selected members of the audience and a panel who would call repeatedly for the army to storm the train. Press home the thought that it was about time something was done. Ask the question - surely the Prime Minister wasn't going to lie down and be made a fool of by these lunatics?

Major social media bloggers were to be recruited to write blog posts supporting a rescue and the newspapers encouraged to give over their front pages to the call to arms. Persons of standing on Twitter, with thousands if not millions of followers were asked to tweet out the hashtags; *#bringinthearmy* *#stormthetrain* as well as the already popular *#freethehostages*.

Crane needed to talk to Harry Poole and Diane Chambers. There wasn't much time to get things rolling, as they needed to hit the deadlines of all the daily newspapers for their overnight production.

The television stations were to be primed and ready for reporting tomorrow's headline. Headlines that would read: the British public were overwhelmingly clamouring for the special forces to go in and rescue the hostages. Even if in reality they weren't, Crane felt sure they would be by tomorrow afternoon. Just in time for the SAS to storm the train.

18:00 hours

Billy approached the toilet with some trepidation, brought on by the smell that greeted him while he was still some way away from it. An understandable if uncomfortable reality of a hijack situation. Services were severely strained. The water used to flush the toilet had long since run out and their precious drinking water was being used sparely, to try and help with the problem of getting rid of human waste. But Billy wasn't there to use the facility, merely to get to his phone.

He closed the door of the tiny cubicle behind him. Squatting down, he opened the cupboard under the sink and was relieved to find the mobile still in place. Powering it up he tapped his foot as he waited for the phone to connect to the network and update itself with any messages waiting for him. He had long since turned off the volume on the phone, so that any new messages would not be announced by a merry tune.

Muttering, "Come on, come one," under his breath, he opened the toilet door just a crack, to make sure no one had noticed he'd gone. From his limited view he could see two hijackers at the far end of the carriage. They looked fairly relaxed and were chatting to each other, telling funny stories by the sound of it, as their laughter drifted over to him. Closing the door with care, he looked back at his phone and was relieved to find a new message.

With the last of his battery he read the missive from Crane. *Storming the train tomorrow night. In the early hours of the morning, 04:00 hours. Be ready.*

As Billy read the words, 'be ready' his battery died, rendering the mobile useless. He couldn't wander over to a hijacker and ask to get his phone charger out of his kit bag. Ever cautious, he returned the now redundant instrument to his hiding place. No point in risking Kourash or his men finding the phone.

Thinking about risks, Billy still wanted to try and get Hazel out of the hell hole they'd found themselves in. But, to be honest, Kourash's stunt of shooting at the helicopter and Colin had put him off. He wondered if Colin had made it, but to be honest if a bullet hadn't killed him, his heart surely would. Billy felt he couldn't try anything that would put Hazel and her baby in harm's way. If she went into labour, then that might be a different matter. For now he'd just have to keep her as calm as possible. And that meant Billy not doing anything stupid.

The best thing to do for now was to make sure they all got down on the floor at the first sign of any arrival of the SAS. Crane had said 04:00, but they needed to be ready before that. Primed to lie on the floor at the first hint of a rescue. Rolling under a seat would be even better. Not only to dodge the bullets that would be flying around, but to stop Kourash or his men grabbing one of them and using that person as a human shield.

The experience onboard the train was wearing down the nerves of the passengers as their captivity dragged on. Billy emerged from the toilet into their tiny carriage which was becoming more tomb-like with each passing day. It was becoming hotter, uncomfortable and filthy, not to mention smelly.

Strangely enough, Billy had to admit, those most deeply affected by fear were the male hostages. He wondered if it was because they were more sensitive to the menacing implications of their plight. It was as if he, Mick and David, considered it their male responsibility to know as much as possible about every new development and debate what dangers it might pose for them. Scraps of overheard talk among their captors or an overheard radio report from the driver's cab, helped them to guess the demands and intentions of Kourash and his men more quickly than the women. Billy decided he would talk to Mick and David and between them agree when the women, and Charlie, would be told of the rescue attempt.

Emma nervously entered the driver's cab, after Kourash's request for her to go to him. Well not so much of a request, as a demand really. She desperately hoped she hadn't done anything wrong. She much preferred his smile to his scowl.

"Emma, my pretty," he said, turning on that 1,000 watt smile. "I wanted to make sure you were alright. After the shooting. I hope it didn't upset you too much."

Emma breathed a sigh of relief. So it was the smiling Kourash who was waiting for her and she returned his smile with gratitude and slumped against him as he put his arms around her.

"Did I frighten you very much?"

Emma nodded against his chest. Suddenly aware of

how much she had actually been frightened by the recent shots and the earlier explosion, despite her show of bravado in the carriage with the other hostages. Tears sprang unbidden to her eyes. She blinked them away, but not before Kourash had seen them and traced the track of one tear with his finger.

"I'm so sorry," he breathed into her ear. "You must remember that I'll never do anything to hurt you. Please believe me," he begged.

Emma struggled to be rational through the web of emotions that were entangling her. The tendrils binding her to Kourash tightening just that little bit more every time she saw him.

"Do you have to do this?" she said. "I'm so afraid that someone is going to get hurt, Kourash."

"Do you mean me?" his lips moved against her cheek as he spoke. "Are you afraid I'm going to get hurt?"

As his lips found hers she finally faced her fear. He was right. She wasn't worried about anyone else on the train, she realised. Just Kourash. She'd do anything to keep him with her. To keep him safe. Just as he would for her.

As his kisses became more passionate, she struggled briefly. Weakly. Not really wanting him to stop. More for show really. But he did stop and pulled slightly away from her.

"What is it, Kourash?" she asked, frantic that she'd done something wrong. Something to offend him. She didn't know much about Muslims. Perhaps what they were doing was wrong in the eyes of his religion? Her hands fluttered against him, plucking at him, her fear rising to the surface again. She was confused. Disoriented. Isolated without his arms around her. She knew emotionally she hadn't coped with this hostage thing very well. At first, all she'd wanted was to be able to go home, to be returned safely to the bosom of her family, to get far away from this madness. When she realised that wasn't going to happen, at least for a long time, she needed reassurance. Guidance. To be told that everything would be alright in the end. Wanted someone to take charge and tell her what to do.

As Kourash's eyes stared through her into her very soul, she knew he understood how she felt. Thankful, she dropped her gaze to the floor. Meekly awaiting his next move.

He took a step away from her, turned the catch on the door to lock it, then quickly returned to embrace her in his arms. Holding her as though he couldn't bear to be apart from her one minute longer.

In the darkened driver's cab, on a train isolated atop a 100' viaduct, Kourash became her father, protector, lover and champion. In all her 19 years, Emma had never felt anything like it.

19:00 hours

Billy's anger was threatening to boil over. Hours of captivity and a feeling of uselessness were making him feel impotent. It seemed that whatever he did either had no effect on their situation, or made things worse. He so desperately wanted to... to... do something. Inactivity was making him irritable and claustrophobic. He wondered why he couldn't dealt with this hijack situation as easily as he'd done with the bullying gang over the weekend.

He slid down in his seat and put his feet up on the opposite one and allowed his mind to drift back. He re-lived the weekend, to see if he could get any inspiration from his earlier success.

Last Saturday night, after a confession from his father that there was 'a bit of trouble' on the estate where his parents lived, Billy had slipped back to the Working Men's Club, where a couple of hours earlier they'd enjoyed a few pints.

Making his way back to the Working Men's Club had been easy. As his eyes had adjusted to the night, his soft soled shoes made no sound and his dark clothes melted into his surroundings, so he hadn't attract any attention from the odd clutches of kids he saw messing around on street corners.

Tony, the Working Men's Club manager, had told him the bar was normally emptying out by about midnight. So feigning tiredness from the long journey, Billy had managed to get his dad out of the pub just before 11pm, after plying him with beer and whisky chasers. It was just after the witching hour when Billy arrived back at the club. Melting into the shadows in the open doorway of the rubbish store, located to the left of the club's entrance, he'd settled down to wait and watch. What he had seen had shocked him. A drunk man had his car stolen, a man's pocket was expertly picked and, the most shocking of all, Tony had been relieved of the night's takings.

After making his excuses to his parents the following night and pretending that he was going back to Aldershot on the train, Billy had crept back to the Working Men's Club hoping that the kids were creatures of habit and would stick to their well practiced modus-operandi. He knew how stupid that was and that it would make them easy to find, but doubted they had thought about it. It would probably never occur to them that, for once, someone would want to find them and might just fight back. Want to make them as afraid as they made their victims.

Billy's thoughts returned to his present situation. If only he could do something to the hijackers to make them feel as afraid as they made the hostages on the train. Take out one or two of them. Help the SAS lads out, by making sure there was at least one less hijacker to deal with when they stormed the train tomorrow night. But would he get a chance? And how could he do anything without a gun?

20:00 hours

Whether it was Billy's contemplation of his exploits over the weekend and his heightened desire to do something, he didn't know, but before he knew it, opportunity knocked. The hijackers were beginning to get very lazy when it came to watching the hostages. They seemed more interested in shouting at Kourash, or chattering about him amongst themselves. Just such a conversation was talking place in front of Billy. The two men had their heads close together, mumbling and grumbling and frequently looking at the door that led to the driver's cab, where Kourash was.

As one of the hijackers moved along the carriage, still chatting to his compatriot, Billy saw his chance. The first man was heading for the toilet. If the second stayed where he was at the top of the carriage, Billy may be able to use the element of surprise and rush him, disabling him and getting his weapon.

Billy elbowed Mick in the side to gain his attention and nodded in the general direction of the lone hijacker, widening his eyes to signal he was going to try something. Mick nodded very slightly in reply and both men watched as the first hijacker reached the toilet. As soon as he had entered the cubicle and closed the door behind him, Billy sprang out of his seat using the momentum of his push-off to quickly close the gap between him and the hijacker. Arm outstretched. Aimed at the man's throat. The combined elements of force and surprise meant the hapless hijacker fell instantly, his body further punished by Billy as he landed on him. Writhing on the floor he was unable to shout for help as his damaged larynx refused to work.

The gun had been involuntarily released from the hijacker's hand and dropped to the floor, where it slid underneath the seats where Emma was sitting. As Billy continued to press his weight onto the stunned hijacker he shouted, "Mick, get the gun! Quick!"

Mick obeyed the instruction immediately, crabbing on his hands and knees towards the seats where the gun lay. But he was older than Billy, with slower reactions and didn't make it in time before someone else picked it up. Emma.

"Well done, Emma," Billy said, craning his neck to see what was happening behind him. As he watched her stand and point the gun at the hijacker on the floor, Billy untangled himself and stood up. "Give the gun to me," he said and reached for it.

Emma's wide eyes blinked in her pale face.

"Emma, quick, before the other one comes back, give the gun to me!" Billy's urgent plea didn't break through whatever was going on in Emma's head. She seemed catatonic. Still the gun was aimed at the hijacker on the floor. Her eyes were wide, pupils dilated. The gun trembled slightly in her hand.

As Billy reached for the gun, the door to the driver's cab opened. Out stepped Kourash. The sight of him seemed to break through Emma's spellbound state. She turned. And pointed the gun at Billy.

"For God's sake, Emma," hissed Billy. "What are you doing?"

"I'd put your hands up, if I were you, Billy. Back up and sit down," Kourash said from the doorway. "You don't want Emma here to shoot you by mistake, do you?"

Billy had no idea what on earth was going on, but as Kourash raised his own gun, Billy was sensible enough to realise that with two guns trained on him, one in the hands of an emotionally deranged girl and one in the hands of an unpredictable mad man, he had no choice but to do as he was told.

Slowly, slowly, he walked backwards and then sank into the nearest seat. But his eyes never left Emma's. Once Billy was seated, Emma seemed to sag, her knees buckling, the gun shaking wildly in her hands.

Kourash stepped over his fallen fellow hijacker and reached Emma's side. Taking the gun out of her hand, he put his arm around her, kissed the top of her head and said, "Thank you, my pretty."

Kourash led Emma away, kicking the injured man back to life as he walked past him. Billy watched them in astonishment. Had he really just seen Emma side with the hijackers?

"Are you okay?" Mick asked him.

"What? Oh, yes, thanks, it just... Emma?"

"I know," Peggy said, joining them. "That poor girl."

"What do you mean that poor girl?" Mick spluttered. "She's gone over to the other side!"

"There must have been a reason for it," Peggy said.

"Yes," agreed Hazel. "She's seemed lonely and sort of isolated from everyone somehow. Maybe she related better to Kourash than she did any of us."

"Well, in that case we've failed her," said Peggy. "We should have done something when we saw the signs."

"She forever had her head in that book," Mick said. "It acted as a barrier. Keeping us all out."

"In Cold Blood," Billy muttered.

"What?" said Mick.

"That's what she was reading. A book about two young men from America who broke into a house and robbed, then killed, the whole family."

"Jesus."

"Talk about life imitating art," said Peggy.

"You're all taking this very well," Billy shook his head. "Aren't you angry? Because I bloody well am."

"Anger won't get us anywhere," said Hazel. "Emma's gone and that's that."

"I suppose you're right," said Billy. "I just hope she'll be okay up there with him," and all three turned to look at the closed driver's cab door.

Day Three
08:00 hours

Crane grabbed his first coffee of the day, a fresh packet of cigarettes and his jacket, before walking out onto the platform of Ribblehead Station. His deep breaths of fresh air brought on a coughing fit. When it subsided, he lit his first cigarette of the day. Looking at the new packet he'd just opened, he wondered if he could keep his consumption down to twenty a day. But there was fat chance of that. As this was his last packet, he'd have to send someone out for supplies.

He'd needed to get out of the waiting room, where the television sets were showing the morning news shows. Each one had appeals on it from family members of the hostages, who had been divided equally between Sky News, BBC News and Good Morning.

The faces might be different, but the stories were the same.

"Please let my wife go. She's pregnant. I'm worried about our unborn baby."

"My Mick never hurt anyone in his life. I don't understand why the hijackers are doing this."

"Please let Peggy go. Tell the hostages her husband

and children need her returned safely."

"My daughter is too young to cope with this on her own. Take me and let her go."

"All I want is my son and husband back. I'm praying every day for their safe return."

The only family not appearing on television was Billy's. It had been decided not to let Billy's parents know that he was on the train. As the authorities couldn't physically stop them talking to people about their son, even though the need for secrecy would be spelled out, no one was willing to take the chance. Crane could only pray there would be a good outcome for Billy. Either way, he would personally apologise to Billy's family for keeping them in the dark. After this was all over.

The hostage's pictures were flashed up on the television screens every few minutes. It was like a wall of death, conjuring up images in Crane's head of when soldiers were killed 'in theatre' and the news channels put up pictures of the fallen.

Articles about the hostages and their families had appeared in every national newspaper. Copies of them all were littered around the waiting room and wherever Crane went, he couldn't get away from their faces. Thank God no one had put them in Keane's broom-cupboard of a shop, where he talked to Kourash. Anyone looking at the pictures couldn't fail to be affected.

Crane was just about ready to return to the fray, when his phone rang. It was his wife, Tina.

"Tom, it's just so awful," she said as soon as he answered her call. "It's all over the television. What's going to happen to those poor people? Will you get them out?"

"I'm sure everything will be fine," Crane said, the platitude sounding trite even to him.

"When is something going to be done about rescuing them?" It seemed Tina wasn't about to stop pressing him for information.

"Look, love, you know I can't talk about anything like that."

"Oh. Sorry. But what about... is he okay?"

"Yes, he's okay."

"Promise?"

"Promise, Tina."

"Alright, but how are you coping? Are you getting enough rest?"

Crane decided only a civilian could ask that question and it made him smile. Even though Tina was an army wife, she still tried to mother him. Tried to look after Crane as she did their son. For once, Crane decided to tell her the truth.

"It's difficult," he admitted. "Sleep is only snatched and doesn't come easily. My head's still buzzing when I lie down. Full of the hijacker's demands, trying to work out what is best for everyone involved and the things I see when I do the supply runs. That's the worst really, the supply runs."

"Why?"

"Because I'm so close, yet so far away," Crane said. "I'm within touching distance of Kourash, but I can't take him out, as we're all unarmed. If we tried anything the other hijacker's would no doubt kill the hostages immediately. And there's always one hostage with Kourash and he's holding a gun to his or her head, so I have to be careful not to react or anger him in any way. So, yes, it's difficult."

"Well it will be, Tom," she said. "But I know you'll

do your best to help get everyone out safely."

"But it's a big ask of the SAS, Tina. Just because everyone is clamouring for the special services to go in, it doesn't mean everyone will make it out alive. Soldiers or hostages."

There. He'd said it. Faced his fear, for by 'everyone' Crane actually meant Billy.

There was a pause before she said, "Then that's something you will have to accept and deal with. Are the odds good?"

"Pretty good," he said.

"Well then, that's the best you can do. Surely it's better than doing nothing."

Crane nodded his agreement, even though Tina couldn't see the gesture. Then, determined to push away negative thoughts and emotions, he said to her, "Look, I've got to go."

"I understand," she said. Whether she did or not, at least the sentiment was there, Crane thought. "Take care of yourself, Tom. Don't do anything stupid."

Crane assured her he wouldn't and after sending a kiss to Daniel, ended the call. He stood on the station platform a few minutes longer. His problem was that he was trying to find a way through the chaos of Kourash's making. So he had to fall back on his training. Follow his orders and try to do his best. Whilst anticipating the worst.

08:30 hours

The new day dawned slowly on the train. Billy and the others trooped in turn to the toilet and tried their best to freshen up. Toothbrushes and other essentials had been sent in, so they had the means of cleaning themselves up. What they lacked was the will to do it.

None of the hostages had been allowed a change of clothes. Another ploy to keep them subdued, to reinforce the fact that Kourash had complete control of them. Controlled what they wore, what they ate and what they drank. He also controlled when they would be allowed to leave the train - if ever.

Emma hadn't been seen since yesterday and Billy wondered if she'd crept into the carriage whilst they were all asleep. Her book had gone and so had her glasses. There was nothing left in the carriage to remind them of her.

According to Crane this was to be their last day on the train. That should have perked Billy up. But strangely it didn't. Billy's brain and body were becoming sluggish. Being imprisoned in the train for the last 48 hours, coupled with the lack of fresh air and exercise was taking its toll.

A rumble from his stomach alerted Billy to the fact that no breakfast had been brought through yet. They'd not been given anything for dinner last night either, so they'd had to resort to eating what was left over from previous meals. Peggy had tried to dole it out equally, but most of them had given Charlie a bit extra out of their own meagre rations.

Billy stood, stretched and decided to find out what was happening. The two hijackers in the carriage were wary of him, after his attempt to grab a gun yesterday, so when Billy approached them, asking to be let through to Kourash, they agreed without hesitation.

As Billy entered the small space, Kourash was on the phone, presumably to the negotiator. Emma looked up as Billy entered and moved away from him, as though she felt the need to put as much space between them as possible. She shrunk into the farthest corner, turning her gaze firmly onto Kourash.

"What are you trying to do?" Kourash spat into the phone. "Why are you hurting your own people like this?"

"Calm down, Kourash, it's just that we've had some logistical problems."

Billy heard the negotiator's voice coming faintly through the receiver Kourash was holding.

"Well sort out your bloody logistical problems and get some food and water sent up to the train. Within the hour."

"Or what?"

"Or I'll start killing hostages. I've had enough of your lies and empty promises."

Kourash slammed down the phone and turned on Billy. "What the fuck do you want?"

"I wanted to know when we'd be getting food and

water, but it seems you're having trouble getting some." Billy had decided to poke the open sore of Kourash's anger.

"It's your bloody negotiator's fault. Not mine. So go back and tell that lot that they'll just have to wait for their food and drink."

"Things not going so well?" Billy smiled. A sardonic grin, rather than a beam.

"Never you mind how things are going," replied Kourash and raised his gun. "Just remember, if the idiot of a negotiator doesn't come up with some supplies, one of you is going to die! So tell that to your friends in the carriage. That'll stop them moaning about food. Instead they can wonder which one of them is about to spend their last hour on this earth."

The gun Kourash was holding was swinging and swaying in his hand as he gesticulated wildly, his eyes wide and staring. His hold on reason was clearly diminishing as the days dragged on, the pressure getting to him. It appeared Kourash was turning into a tin pot dictator, losing his grip on reality and over estimating his power. But that, of course, made him even more dangerous. Even more of a threat, as far as the hostages were concerned.

Billy put his hands up and backed away. "Okay, okay, I'm going," he said and retreated through the doorway. His message to his fellow captors would be that breakfast should arrive in about an hour. He was going to keep the accompanying threat to himself.

He was still concerned about Emma. She had very deliberately not looked at him whilst he was in the driver's cab. But her body was stiff and she seemed uncomfortable in Billy's presence. Displaying guilt? Regret? Billy hoped so, but couldn't be sure. Still it was her decision to make, to side with Kourash, so she'd just have to face any consequences brought on by her actions.

But on the other hand... she was so young. A pampered and cosseted young girl who had no idea what terrible things went on in the world. It was as if she were playing out the role of Truman Capote in the bloody stupid book she was reading. Billy had skipped through it while Emma was enjoying one of her prolonged visits with Kourash. He now realised that Emma was reading the book that he vaguely remembered was chronicled in the film 'Capote'. In the film, it was clear Truman Capote made the killers think he was their friend, in order to get close to them and to be able to write about them from a position of authority. He didn't actually want to befriend them, just wanted their secrets. But Billy wondered if Emma had gotten the wrong end of the stick and wasn't pretending to be close to Kourash. But was actually spellbound by his looks, his air of authority and commitment to his cause. If that were the case, through her naivety, she warranted Billy's pity, not anger.

Crane had returned to the command centre, just in time to hear Keane's conversation with Kourash.

"You are going to send in supplies, aren't you?" he asked Keane after he finished talking to Kourash.

"Of course. I just don't want him to think he has the upper hand. I want him to realise he can't make demands and get everything he wants."

"But now he's threatening to kill a hostage if he doesn't get food and fresh water."

"I know that, don't worry, it's just posturing," Keane tried to reassure Crane, who wasn't convinced. "It's like a chess game," Keane continued. "We make our next move, based on the previous move of the adversary."

"That's all very well if you have a sane partner to play with. Kourash is far from sane and completely unpredictable."

"Please, Crane. I do know what I'm doing,"

"I bloody well hope so."

"Stop it, Sgt Major," Booth snapped. "Keane is doing a very difficult job under extreme circumstances. Don't make things harder by criticising him. I understand that your normal demeanour is to pick the bones out of every situation, that's why you are an investigator. But this is a different situation entirely. Perhaps if you were to shut up and observe, you might learn something. Now go and get ready to deliver the supplies."

The rebuke stung. But Crane could see the old man had a point. So he put his hands up in mock surrender and went to help load the supplies onto the truck. Time would tell who was right. But in the meantime Crane was certainly learning new skills in manipulation and negotiation. And that wasn't such a bad thing, he had to admit.

09:00 hours

The familiar rumble of the truck on the track, heralding new supplies, was greeted with anticipation by the hostages.

"I wonder what's for breakfast," Hazel mused.

"I hope it's those croiss, croisssss... what are they dad?" Charlie asked.

"Croissants, son."

"Oh yeah, that's right, croissants. I liked those." David jiggled up and down in his seat. "Do we have any jam left, Peggy? They were really scrummy with jam."

Peggy smiled at the boy and went to the food supplies heaped in a jumble on a spare table between four empty seats. As she was sorting through the tins and jars, under the watchful eye of a hijacker's gun, Kourash burst into the carriage.

"David!" he shouted. "Come here."

"What? Why? Billy? What's going on?"

"Never mind what's going on, I need you up here to help," said Kourash.

"But, but, Billy normally does that. Help with the supplies."

"Well today's not normal so fucking get a move on."

Kourash was clearly losing patience with David, so Billy intervened. "Kourash, please..."

"And you can fuck off as well," snapped Kourash, swinging his gun around to train it on Billy. Billy opened his mouth to reply, but Hazel grabbed his arm.

"Sit down, Billy, there's nothing you can do."

As Billy acceded to her request, he watched as David was grabbed roughly by one of the hijackers, his hands grasping either side of David's jacket as he pulled him up and out of his seat. Another prised Charlie's fingers off his dad's arm. A protesting David was bundled into the driver's cab, into Kourash's clutch, all the time followed by his son's wails. As the hijacker moved away, Billy and the others could see through the open driver's door. Kourash and David were stood slightly back from the opening. The wind blew Kourash's curls, whipping them around his shoulders like writhing snakes. He held David by the collar of his stained and worn shirt with one hand. The other hand held a pistol which was pressed to David's head.

Peggy grabbed Charlie as he attempted to run to his father. He was crying and screaming hysterically, "Dad! Dad! I want my dad!"

Charlie tried his best to wriggle out of Peggy's embrace, desperate to reach his father. But she was too quick for him. Enfolding him in a bear hug, she held him close, bending her head to whisper in his ear.

"It's alright. Dad will come back. He'll only be a little while," and she led him to a seat where Charlie's screams subsided into heartbreaking sobs. Billy could only watch and hope Peggy was right.

The supplies were brought on board, under the watchful eye of Kourash, who never once relaxed his grip on David's clothes, nor took the pistol away from

David's head. When the exchange was finished and the delivery truck was rumbling its way backwards along the tracks, the supplies were brought into the carriage and placed on a table. The enticing smell of freshly ground coffee filled the carriage and Billy realised how much he needed his morning caffeine fix.

Hazel stood, grabbed some paper cups and started to pour the coffee for them. Peggy had managed to get Charlie to stop crying with the promise of a croissant. Mick stood, complaining that his stomach was rumbling and he needed food before he wasted away, bringing the expected laughs from his fellow hostages. As they all relaxed and settled down with their breakfast, Billy fully expected David to be brought back into the carriage. Instead Kourash lifted the phone.

"Keane," Kourash shouted, so they all could hear him, his voice floating down the carriage aisle. "Watch your monitors."

Placing the receiver on the control panel, Kourash didn't cut the call. From his seat near the driver's cab, Billy could hear Keane's ineffectual squawks coming out of the telephone. The negotiator reduced to a tame parrot, churning out his trite phrases.

Very much afraid that things were about to go badly wrong, Billy stood, this time ignoring Hazel's protests. He moved towards the open door, only to be stopped by an AK47 pushed into his chest by a hijacker. A sign for him to stop right where he was and to back off. But Billy stood his ground, refusing to move away, his gaze drawn to David in the open driver's cab doorway. The one facing the media field. The awful tableau no doubt being beamed across the world as Kourash paused dramatically for a few seconds. Then he pushed David out of the cab, to fall 100' to his death, as though David meant no more to him than a discarded toy that he was throwing away in fit of childish temper.

David's sickening scream echoed around the majestic Dales, joined by his son's. Their voices locked together until their duet was broken by a barely audible thud, as David hit the ground.

Kourash held his arms aloft, complete with gun in one hand. A gesture of defiance. A clear message to the world that he was in charge. He then bowed slightly, as though acknowledging an enthralled audience, before closing the door, cutting them off from the outside world once again.

Picking up the handset Kourash said into it, "Perhaps that will teach you to stop playing games with me, Keane."

09:15 hours

There was a beat of absolute silence before the waiting room erupted.

"Get those pictures off the television," screamed the Colonel to Dudley-Jones. "I can't believe they just showed that."

"With respect, sir, they didn't know what Kourash was going to do. They are beaming live pictures, remember," said Dudley-Jones.

"I don't care how the bloody hell they're beaming, just get those pictures off the air."

"I'm probably best placed to do that," the grey man said and Hardwick retrieved his mobile from his pocket and walked out casually, as though he was in complete control. Crane could only hope he was.

"What about the internet, DJ?" Crane asked, as the Colonel answered a call on his mobile.

"It's all over it, sir. We'll try and get some of the sites shut down until they stop showing the hostage falling to his death," Dudley-Jones grabbed a tissue and wiped his sweat streaked face. "We're trying our best, sir."

Crane placed his hand on the young Intelligence

Operative's shoulder. "I know, lad. You're all doing a great job. And as for you, it's a big responsibility being the sole intelligence link here, receiving all the information, passing it on to us dinosaurs and then relaying instructions back to the team."

Just then Crane and Dudley-Jones were interrupted by Hardwick, who had finished his call and returned to the waiting room. "The Prime Minister wants to speak to us. Open a secure satellite line, Dudley-Jones, he wants a video call."

Crane moved away from Dudley-Jones so he could get on with his job without interference. As the screen on the wall started to fizz and crackle, everyone moved into a clear viewing position. Keane came out of his cubby-hole, to stand next to Crane and Hardwick.

As the picture broke up into pixels and then cleared, the Prime Minister could be seen, looking rather more tousled than Crane had ever seen him before. He had no jacket on. His shirt sleeves were rolled up and tie off. He ran his hand through hair that Crane was sure had more grey in it than last week and began to speak.

"I wanted to take this opportunity to personally thank you all for your efforts. I've been kept fully up to date on the negotiations and diplomatic liaison, by members of COBRA. But after this latest incident," his voice cracked for just a moment, "I'm afraid I've been left with no choice. You have all done a wonderful job of containing the hijackers, looking after the hostages and providing real time intelligence that has helped tremendously. However, after much internal debate and under advisement from the Chiefs of Staff Committee, I've decided that Kourash has left us with no choice."

Crane thought it interesting that the Prime Minister spat Kourash's name, showing his feelings for the man.

Crane was sure every person in the room concurred.

"We will go in tonight, or rather tomorrow morning at 04:00 hours. I can't give the hijackers time to kill another hostage, nor the opportunity to negotiate a peaceful settlement to the incident. They've burned their bridges as it were. There is now no way back.

"Obviously this statement must be kept confidential. It is essential we maintain our element of surprise. For now we have to maintain contact with the hijackers and try and keep Kourash as stable as possible. I know this is probably an impossible task, but I urge you to try. Let's not give him further cause to retaliate.

"Once again, thank you and I hope you will join me in praying for the safe rescue of the remaining hostages."

Crane wondered if they were all going to bow their heads, with the Prime Minister leading prayers in sombre tones, but to his relief the satellite feed went dead and everyone relaxed.

"We've just had confirmation that the three big television stations, BBC, ITV and Sky have agreed that the pictures are too distressing to show and none of them will show the incident again," Dudley Jones said. "However, there are other stations, such as Aljazeera, who are refusing to comply. And it's still all over the internet and now there are tweets about it, providing the internet links to the video. We're trying our best to contain it, but I'm afraid you all need to understand that it's an impossible task."

"Very well," Booth replied.

"Still, the bright side of this is that it will help our cause in turning public opinion," said Crane. "Even more people will now be calling for the hijacking to end. For the armed forces to do something about it. I know it seems a heartless thing to say, but Kourash may just have done us all a favour."

Crane mentally crossed his fingers and prayed that what he'd just said would come true. Why on earth did it have to come to this, though? An innocent man, hurled out of a train would be the catalyst for turning public opinion. There would be those who would say that therefore David's death had not been in vain. But Crane doubted that would be of much comfort to David's wife. Or to David's son.

The screams of those on board the train were more terrible than David's scream as he hurtled to his death, if that were at all possible. Billy and Mick leapt at the hijackers, but were turned away by threatening gestures from their guns and by Kourash shooting at the ceiling. A clear sign to do as they were told, or else. The women were frantic, their shattering screaming filling Billy's head.

Unable to get to Kourash and pummel him to death, Billy turned to do the only thing he could. Try and help his fellow hostages. He went to sit next to Hazel, cradling her, encouraging her to calm down. He told her she needed to think of the baby. No one wanted to have to deliver her child here in this filthy carriage. It was vital she calmed down for the baby's sake, as well as Billy's nerves. His last words bringing the reward of a small smile.

Billy looked up and saw that Mick had gone to help Peggy try and calm down Charlie. Jesus. What would the violent death of his father do to the poor child, Billy wondered and once more his anger began to build. The fucking bastard. Kourash couldn't be allowed to get away with this.

Billy stood, saw that the other hijackers were jabbering amongst themselves at the opposite end of the carriage and took his opportunity. He burst into the driver's cab, to find Kourash puffed up like a peacock. Strutting around the small space, chest out, gun raised, praising Allah. Billy turned away from the posturing idiot and went towards Emma, who was cowering in the corner. He crouched down beside her.

"Billy, Billy, did that really just happen? I saw Kourash push David out of the door. Is he dead? I, I..." her voice faltered and became hiccupping sobs. "I'm sorry, sorry, I didn't realise what he was like. What are we going to do?" Emma clung to Billy. "Are we all going to die?"

Billy really couldn't answer that question. He held Emma slightly away from him, so he could see her face. "We've just got to hang on, Emma," he said, trying hard to inject steel into his voice. Trying not to display his own horror and fear.

"Can... can... I come back with you?" she pleaded. "I'm sorry about earlier, I don't want to stay here, please don't make me, please let me come back."

Billy nodded his agreement, for what else could he do? He couldn't leave her in Kourash's clutches. He helped her to her feet. At the doorway he called for Hazel to come and take Emma from him. Once free of the deluded teenager, as he would now always think of Emma, he turned to Kourash.

"Proud of yourself now, are you?" he spat.

"Most definitely," Kourash smiled. "I've just sent a clear message that I will not be messed about by anyone. Not by the negotiator, the British Government, nor the Afghan Government. Now they all know what they are dealing with. A man true to his cause."

Kourash hit his chest with a clenched fist. "A man not afraid to make the ultimate sacrifice in order to ensure his demands are met."

The fire of jihad was in Kourash's eyes. Billy knew he couldn't do anything to change Kourash's mind, but he'd have his say anyway.

"You haven't made the ultimate sacrifice," yelled Billy. "David did!"

Kourash sneered in reply. "Well in that case his family should be pleased and treat him like a hero. David has now stood out from the greyness of his humdrum ordinary life. He will be remembered down the ages as someone who died for his country."

"But what about Charlie?" Billy rounded on the man he could only think was a complete lunatic. "What about him? He's only a child. Just think what a terrible effect his will have on him. How badly he could be affected by these terrible events."

"And I should care about that?" countered Kourash. "That's nothing compared to what I've had to live through. Abandoned, effectively orphaned. Taken in by a family who cared little for my welfare and showed me no affection. I had to put up with the hand that life dealt me. So will Charlie. Now go away and leave me alone."

Kourash pushed Billy out of the door and slammed it shut. An evil king left alone in his throne room.

10:00 hours

"Right lads, listen up," Major Blunt of the Special Air Services (SAS) spoke in a quiet calm voice, but it was a voice that was immediately obeyed.

The troop of 15 casually dressed soldiers, stilled. They lounged in seats, sat on top of tables or stood leaning against the wall. Despite their nonchalance, each one was focused on the man they called 'the old man'. Their squadron leader.

"If there was any doubt before, there is little doubt now," he began. "We're going in."

Murmurings of agreement were accompanied by much nodding of heads. At last, they seemed to say.

"Okay, settle down," Blunt continued and was immediately obeyed with much smiling. "There will be two plans, dependent upon weather. Plan A, if there is low cloud and rain, as forecast, we'll use aircraft support first. Creating immediate 'shock and awe' as the Yanks say."

As the laughter faded, he continued. "However, if it's a clear, still moonlit night, Plan B will be implemented. With no initial air support. The hijackers would see the planes coming from a mile away and would more than likely kill all hostages before you had a chance to reach the train. Both plans call for the Special Projects Team of the SAS to go in first. That's you lot. Just in case you've forgotten who you are, as you've had to wait so long for the all clear to go in and get the job done."

The men laughed again, as expected. They knew the old man liked his jokes.

"Right, Captain Thomas here will explain," and he made way for their leader, the Boss. The man who would lead the operation, who would stand shoulder to shoulder with them. The man whom they would follow anywhere and do anything for. Captain Thomas was a Troop Leader in the Special Projects Team, a wing of the SAS specialising in anti-terrorist and counter-terrorism. The Captain and his lads undertook training, in rotation, in hostage rescue, siege breaking, and live firing exercises.

"For both plans," he began, "we have to be in place at the bottom of the viaduct arches. Therefore we'll go in at approximately 21:00 hours tonight, when the last supplies of the day are taken to the train. The hijackers will be busy watching the truck and loading stores, so we'll come in from the back, at ground level, ready and waiting to scale the arches just before the raid begins. The delivery will be slightly later than usual, to ensure we can go in under cover of darkness. The last thing we want is the media showing live pictures of us crawling into position. Pictures which are no doubt being monitored by the hijackers.

"We'll have to wait there, under cover, at the bottom of the arches, until five minutes before kick-off. Then we'll scale the walls using the latest 'geko' suction technology. No need for ropes or grappling hooks, not that you could swing one 100' high. We used it when we put the listening devices under the train carriages, so we know it works. Only this time you'll be carrying extra weight as you'll be fully loaded. So just be careful and take your time.

"At the appointed hour, you will split into two factions. One going inside the train, the other climbing onto the roof. The hijackers regularly patrol the top of the train, so we'll need to make that area secure. Just in case extra support is needed, another unit will be waiting in helicopters to drop onto the track or the roof of the train, where ever back up is needed."

"We've been training with the replica of the two carriage train with marks where we think people are. This has been done in daylight so you now know the exact layout. But as the movement of the passengers and hijackers is fluid, we'll continue training today using every variable we can come up with. The carriages are now blacked out with film over the windows and will be filled with smoke and noise in an exact reproduction of what you'll be faced with tonight."

Thomas indicated a two carriage train, complete with driver's cab that was in the large warehouse structure they were all standing in. Instead of building a hardboard replica it had been decided it was quicker and easier to use a similar real train. Northern Rail had kindly provided an old train, no longer in service, located at one of their repair yards. So the whole team had moved out of the barracks, setting up a base camp in the secluded Northern Rail location. There wouldn't be any likelihood of the old train ever being used again. Already there were many bullet holes in the structure and the seats had been shredded by strafing fire.

"We'll practice the plan over and over," he

continued, "until your movements are automatic, your reflexes sharp and you manage the whole operation without killing any bloody hostages. Right?"

"Yes, sir!" the answer rang out. The enthusiasm, the anticipation of the adrenaline rush to come filling every man in the room.

"Very well. Let's get on with it. Dismissed."

11:00 hours

"So," Keane said, "are you proud of yourself now? Have you gained enough notoriety?"

"Well, the news was getting a bit stale, so I thought I'd give the media something to report, instead of just saying that we are at deadlock."

Kourash's humour was distasteful to Keane and he gave vent to his anger.

"What the bloody hell was the point of killing David? You'd already got what you wanted."

"Got what I wanted? Got what I wanted? Of course I haven't. I want my brother released from Bagram now! That's what I want, you imbecile."

"Well, that's out of my hands, Kourash. I can only ask. If the people in power keep saying 'no', what am I to do?"

"You weak, ineffectual man. Call yourself a negotiator? You couldn't negotiate your way out of a paper bag," Kourash's voice dripped with distain. He continued in the same vein, "How many people have you gotten killed? Have you ever talked anyone out of a hostage situation without casualties?"

Each drip was a further blow on Keane's already

battered and bruised psyche, leaving him unable to speak.

Gathering what little fight he had left, Keane said, "Look Kourash, the best offer I can make is that if you let the hostages go, we'll get as many as we can out of prison."

"No."

"Come on, Kourash, you know how it works, you give me something and I'll give you something."

"Yes, well, your record on that score isn't very good is it? So far you've managed to get a delivery man shot, a helicopter shot down, a carriage blown up and a hostage thrown off the viaduct. Strangely enough, I just don't believe you anymore. Every time you've promised something you've failed to deliver."

"Come on, Kourash, be sensible. What about letting the pregnant woman go. Hazel isn't it?" Keane's hands were shaking, but he was determined not to allow that shake to be heard in his voice. "Think how much good publicity you'd get from that simple act."

"In the name of Allah, Keane, I said no and I mean no. Anyway you lot aren't the only ones who can change public opinion."

"What are you talking about, Kourash? What do you mean?" but Keane was talking into a dead instrument. Kourash had terminated the phone call.

Keane slumped over the desk in the shop, his head in his hands and wondered how he'd get through the next 17 hours until the raid. Trying to contain Kourash was virtually impossible.

The door opened and Crane walked in. "You alright?" he asked.

Keane huffed, "I don't think I know what 'alright' is anymore, Crane," he admitted. "My emotional reserves are running low. I'm going to struggle to get through this. I don't know what to do next."

"I agree with you there, not knowing what move to make next," Crane said. "How do you placate a madman?"

Keane thought back over his training and his experience. "One train of thought is to appease him by agreeing to whatever he wants. Agreeing with his demands would diffuse the situation to some extent. Buy us a bit more time."

"Until he realises you're lying again."

"Yes, there's the rub. I can't give him what he really wants. His brother released from Bagram Detention Centre."

"So he still doesn't know his brother's dead?"

"No and I can only hope he doesn't find out before 4am tomorrow morning. If he does..."

"He'll kill them all," Crane finished the sentence for him.

12:00 hours

Constance Thornton sat in front of the television in her home in Birmingham. Two other women alternated wandering around the house with her or sitting down with her. Her sister Brenda and her mother. But Constance didn't want to talk to either of them. Just wanted to watch the television. The endless cycle that was the 24 hour news programmes. When one started reporting a different story, she would change channels to get the picture of the train back up on the screen. The train from which her husband had been thrown to his death. The train her son was still on.

Her mother tried to prise the remote control from her hands, saying, "Come on, love, turn that off for a while, you need a rest."

But Constance didn't need a rest. Wouldn't. Couldn't. Not until her son was returned safely to her. So she sat in the clothes she had worn for the third day now, in front of the never ending stream of pictures from the Ribblehead Viaduct. Occasionally her lank black hair fell into her eyes and she pushed it away subconsciously. She could smell the sweat emanating from her. She needed a shower. But didn't have time to take one. She might miss something on the news.

Her sister walked into the room with a mug a tea. "Hey, honey," she said, fake gaiety in her voice. "Here's a nice cup of tea, with lots of sugar in it."

When Constance didn't take her eyes from the television set, Brenda tried again. "Constance, here," she said and pushed the mug into Constance's hands.

Looking down at the mug, Constance frowned in disgust and put it on the low table in front of her, to join several other mugs of tea that she hadn't drunk. Tea wouldn't make her feel better. The only thing that would, was Charlie's safe return. She'd prayed and prayed for it.

"Oh, Constance," Brenda started to say, but she was cut short by a whistling tune from the mobile phone that Constance had dropped and left, ignored, on the floor.

"Here, love," Brenda said, retrieving it. "You better see who that is."

Constance shook her head. "No, I'm watching the television, get out of the way. I might miss something."

With a sigh, Brenda opened the protective mobile phone wallet and pressed the message button. Frowning, Brenda's mouth moved as she silently read the text.

"What is it? Is it about Charlie?" Constance asked as Brenda held out the phone to her.

"Here, I think you better read this yourself."

As Constance read the beginning of the text, she fell off the settee and onto her knees, as if continuing her constant prayers. Prayers that might just have been answered.

If you don't want Charlie to go the same way as David, this is what you have to do...

Joyce Harrison was also glued to the television. Still clad in crumpled, dirty, pyjamas at mid-day, she had ignored the earlier pleas from her husband to go and have a nice shower or bath. He said it would make her feel better. Joyce knew that the only thing that would make her feel better was the safe return of Emma.

He'd just gone off to work. Enraged, Joyce had turned on him before he left, screaming out her fear and pain, "You heartless bastard, don't you care about Emma?"

"Of course I do, you stupid woman," he'd retorted. "It's just that I refuse to fall to pieces and sit had home moaning and crying. Just look at yourself," he sneered. "You disgust me. I can't wait to get away from you. If there's any news of Emma, the police know how to contact me."

The last thing she'd heard was the slamming of the front door, as he'd gone off to his precious office. All dressed up in his best suit. Gone off to his precious mistress, more like, Joyce realised. Which made her feel just as bad as she felt about Emma.

It was an hour later that she was roused out of her trance-like state by the message notification on her mobile phone. Grasping for it, like a hardened smoker would grab at a pack of cigarettes after not having had a nicotine fix for many hours, Joyce pulled the message up on the screen of her phone.

If you want to see your daughter alive again, follow these instructions...

Anything, she thought, I'll do anything to see Emma alive and read the rest of the message.

Mark Richards was in the garden, digging frantically, trying to dislodge an old tree he'd meant to get rid of ages ago. Peggy had mentioned it a few times, but he'd always put the job off. So he'd decided to do it now. For Peggy. So she'd see what he'd done for her when she got home. He should have put some shoes on, he realised. His slippers were useless when it came to putting his foot on the spade, to provide extra force. All they were achieving was making the bottom of his feet sore and bruised.

The worst part of all this was the waiting, waiting, waiting. He'd never before felt so helpless, he realised, as he wiped the sweat from his forehead, smearing it with dirt as he did so. All he wanted was for Peggy to come home. Was that too much to ask for?

Their two children, even though they were now teenagers, needed their mother, just as much as he needed his wife. They were handling this remarkably well, but Mark was afraid that once this was all over, they'd fall apart. He'd practically pushed them out of the door that morning, insisting they go to college. They'd be better off with their friends than with their distant, distraught father.

He had to stay strong for his family. He dug his spade savagely into the hard earth. He really should have left this until tomorrow. Rain was forecast for tonight, which would soften the ground, making the job easier. But Mark didn't want the job made easier. The harder the better. He had to gain control over the resistant earth, as there was nothing else that he could control in his life at the moment.

As he stepped back from the flower bed for a breather, his mobile phone rang. Hoping the kids were alright, he eagerly pulled it out of his pocket and nearly fell over when he read the message. Holding onto the spade with one hand and his phone with the other,

Mark read over and over:
Do you love Peggy? To get her back you have to...

David Mountford was at work. Staring at his computer screen. Seeing not the information contained on it, but a picture of his wife, heavily pregnant, trapped on a train. Terrified. Alone. Hoping the baby wouldn't be born early.

He got up and left his cubicle, walking to the gents toilets. Once there, he looked at himself in the mirror. Not usually known for his dapper attire, crisp white shirts and well pressed suits, what he was wearing that day was particularly bad, even for him. His suit was crumpled. Well, it wasn't really a suit, as David realised he'd put on mismatched trousers and jacket. He hadn't changed his socks and he'd had the same shirt on for two days now. Two days of insane fear, unable to concentrate on anything but Hazel.

He'd gone into work because he couldn't stand the empty house anymore. The nursery they'd just finished. The empty cot mocking him so much that he'd not been upstairs for the last 48 hours. But work offered no respite either. His boss generously accepting that he was completely unfit for work, but needed the familiarity of the surroundings.

David was just about to leave the toilets and go and get his fifth coffee of the day, when his mobile buzzed. A message. Trying to open his phone with fumbling fingers, all he managed to do was to drop it.

He sat down heavily on the floor and retrieved it. With a shaking finger, he pressed the button to read the message.

If you want Hazel back and your baby delivered safely you will need to...

Rita Smith was talking to her neighbour from her back step, having opened the front door a couple of minutes ago, to peer down the street, to see if any police cars were coming with a message for her. A message that would tell her that Mick was alright and coming home. Even bringing him home. She didn't dare to think about that too much, but it was what she was hoping for. Sleep had been impossible the last two nights and she'd paced her way around the house, watched the television news, read every newspaper she could find and cleaned the house to gleaming perfection. After all she didn't want Mick coming back to a dirty house.

"I never thought driving a train could be so dangerous," she confided over the back fence to Joan, her neighbour for the past 20 years. Pulling off her rubber gloves she said, "I know he gets things like trees on the track and he once had someone jump in front of his train. That shook him, I can tell you. But it was only the once. And he handled it well. My Mick's a strong 'un that's for sure."

"Isn't he due to retire soon?" Joan asked.

"Yes, he's only got another couple of years. Don't know what he's going to do then, though. Not one for keeping still is my Mick."

"Have the kids been in touch?"

"Oh yes, phone me all the time they do."

"They haven't come up then?"

"Well, you know how it is," Rita replied, studying the tiny back garden. "They've got their families, jobs, you know... really busy they all are... but they're ringing me. Can't expect more than that, can I?" Rita was perilously close to tears, for the umpteenth time that morning.

A buzzing sound cut through her distress and she

put her hands in the pocket of the apron she was wearing.

"Expect that's one of them now," she said proudly to Joan as she opened the message box.

"Rita? Are you alright?" Joan leaned over the waist high fence grabbing Rita as she swayed on her feet.

"What? Yes, yes I am. Look at this. Mick's going to be okay!"

Mick will be allowed to leave the train if you do as I say...

14:00 hours

The latest background on the hijackers, made uncomfortable reading. Crane had taken the paperwork outside into the blustery afternoon to read it, feeling the need of a nicotine crutch.

Dudley-Jones' notes were concise and succinct. It appeared that the Islamic State of Iraq and al-Sham (Isis or just IS as they were becoming known) wasn't just battling its way into the cities of Iraq, it was also fighting for global support and action via a major social media campaign, backed up by slick videos, which were being used to call for support from abroad. This is how Kourash had been seduced into their ranks and no doubt how many more like him would be in the future.

In the videos, the Isis leader, al-Baghdadi called for 'Sunni youths' to join the Isis jihad. "I appeal to the youths and men of Islam around the globe and invoke them to mobilise and join us to consolidate the pillar of the state of Islam and wage jihad against the rafidhas (Shia), the safadis of Shi'ites. Proudly support the Muslim cause and fully support Isis," he'd said.

Supporting this video were hosts of others, in different languages. And it wasn't just French and

Arabic languages that were being used to recruit support for the Isis campaign - videos were appearing with English translations as well.

According to the officials and security experts, there was a growing danger that Islamists would look to radicalising more recruits from Britain. It was what might happened when they returned to Britain, that mostly worried the security services. MI5 estimated that there were potentially hundreds of young men due to return to the UK from the jihad, who could be sufficiently radicalised to consider bringing the fight to their homeland. Clearly Kourash belonged to this new breed of terrorist, Crane realised. God help us if there are more like him, he thought.

Folding up the paperwork and taking a turn along the platform, Crane knew that this information only served to strengthen the Government's resolve that they mustn't give in. The Prime Minister had stressed time and time again during this siege, that he must show the hijackers that the British won't negotiate with terrorists. Crane had asked Hardwick if that meant even at the expense of the hostages. If necessary, had been the reply. He'd said it was better for the common good. Better to lose a few now than many more in the future. But would that strong stance against negotiations stop the terrorists trying again in the future? No one seemed to have an answer to that question. Crane pondered that it didn't seem to have stopped anyone trying so far. If it had made any difference to the fanatics planning their campaigns of terror, it just meant that they used suicide bombers instead.

So the British people were behind the Prime Minister and the prayers of a nation were being offered up, asking for a quick end to the siege. Praying for the safe return of the hostages. But would they all be returned safely? Crane hoped so, but was pragmatic enough to accept that there may well be casualties. On both sides. Everyone on that train was a human being. It was as though they were praying for one set of human beings to die, so that another group could live and Crane didn't feel comfortable with that. Not at all. So he let others do the praying.

His head was starting to spin with all the introspection, so he was relieved when a shout rang out, calling him back into the waiting room.

As he walked back in, everyone was once again glued to the television screens. Which were full of images of the hostage's families. Begging, pleading, crying, entreating. Wanting the Government to give in to the demands of Kourash and let the prisoners in Bagram go free, so that their son, husband, father, mother, or daughter, would be released.

Over and over looped the insistent voices, filling the airwaves with their distress. Dudley-Jones replaced the telephone he had been talking into and gave a strangled cough, which Crane took as an attempt to get their attention.

"Yes, DJ?"

"Sir, I've just spoken to the team. It seems the hostage's families started bombarding the news broadcasting companies about an hour ago. Demanding to be heard, wanting to appear on television. It appears they've decided not to comply with our request to keep themselves out of the media as much as possible."

"Or been persuaded not to comply," growled Crane.

"Exactly, sir."

"What do you make of this, Keane?"

"Doesn't surprise me. Kourash has the hostage's

mobile phones. It wouldn't take a genius to come up with an idea to make full use of them."

"I expect this will make the Prime Minister feel rather uncomfortable," said the civil servant.

"Best you get on the phone then, pull in a few more favours from the media and stop this poisonous rubbish. The SAS lads are going in tonight," said Booth "and I'll not have them made scapegoats. The Prime Minister wants cheers for them, not criticism. And what the Prime Minister wants, the Prime Minister gets, don't forget." The Colonel was clearly in a strident mood and Crane smiled to himself.

"As if I could forget," the man in the grey suit said and moved outside to make his calls.

"Fucking politicians," said Booth.

"Amen to that," agreed Crane, forgetting about his earlier promise to himself to leave God out of it.

15:00 hours

An hour later and the hostage's families were still pleading for the safe return of their loved ones. They had demands this time, they said. They were demanding that the government give Kourash what he wanted. They were still on every television channel, saying that they refused to be quiet any longer. Saying the authorities couldn't stop them speaking out. They'd decided to join in the call for action - but action that would mean the hijackers would let their loved ones go. Action that involved opening the gates of Bagram Detention Centre. Peaceful action, they stressed, not violent action.

Harry and Diane were debating who was right. Those calling for the army to go in, or those calling for the hijacker's demands to be met.

"In theory, both should result in their loved ones being released," Diane said to Harry.

"Well, yes, but can Kourash be believed and trusted? Would he really let everyone go? On the other hand he could do the ultimate. Blow everyone up."

"I see what you mean," replied Diane. "He's already blown up one carriage hasn't he?" and they both turned to look at the hulk of twisted metal that could be clearly seen on the tracks and the pieces of shrapnel that littered the ground underneath the viaduct.

"Exactly. And how can you trust someone who fired a gun at a rescue helicopter?"

"Mmm, but I can understand the families want someone to listen to their voices. They must feel that no one is."

"But it's swaying public opinion again, so we have to rally round the troops as it were and get everyone back on the social media campaign. If Crane's right and Kourash has put the families up to it and is manipulating these poor desperate people, then we'll have to beat the hijackers at their own game and standing around talking won't achieve that."

"Yes, sir," grinned Diane and gave a mock salute before ducking away and pulling out her tablet.

Since the hostages had made their appeals on television, Keane had not contacted Kourash, preferring to wait and see how long it would take for Kourash to snap and call him. It took just over an hour.

"Have you seen the television, Keane?"

"Which channel would that be?"

"You know which channel. All the news channels. Stop trying to be clever."

"Oh, you mean the hostage's families?"

"Yes. Well?"

"Well what?"

"Are you listening to them? Are you going to do anything?"

"Oh, that. Sorry, meant to tell you, we should have news by tomorrow. At the moment the Afghani government are drawing up a list of those who will be released. They've promised the list for 9 am UK time tomorrow."

"At long bloody last, I knew that would…"

Keane cut the call in the middle of Kourash's sentence.

"Jesus, Keane, should you be doing that? Isn't he unstable enough as it is?" Crane had been stood next to Keane in the shop, listening in.

"I want to keep his mind occupied on the release for tomorrow morning. I don't need to let him gloat. If I act disinterested, then he's going to think he's won. Think that I won't discuss it because I've had to back down. Which is good for him. So now all he'll be thinking about is how he's got one over on the British Government and that his brother will be released tomorrow."

"You're a fucking good liar, Keane. You had me going," Crane nodded his head in approval.

"I know, Crane, but hey what can you do?" Keane grinned for the first time in a long time and Crane saw a flash of the man he'd met three days ago. He could only hope that after some well earned R&R, Keane would become that man again.

18:00 hours

By early evening, the rescue was on. Low clouds had come scurrying across the vast vista of the Yorkshire Dales. Drizzle cloaked the train, softening its hard edges. From the media field it was like looking through a room full of cobwebs, à la Miss Haversham. She had waited in her house, stuck in a time warp for many years. The train had only been there three days, but that was three days too long.

Crane watched as the news editors of the UK television stations and newspapers were being briefed. The rescue mission would take place at 04:00 hours tomorrow morning, but troops would be making their way to designated spots overnight. So absolutely no live pictures of the train tonight. No indication if what was to come, no speculation as to when a rescue might take place. Library pictures only please.

The Prime Minister's press secretary continued, "I am sure none of you want to be responsible for a massacre. A massacre of the hostages, that is, by the hijackers, should they get even a whiff of what is to come. You all know how unstable the minds of the hijackers are and therefore by default how unstable the whole situation is. Deaths have already occurred. Please do not be responsible for any more. Your co-operation is vitally important. Kourash is monitoring all the news stations and newspapers through the internet via a secure satellite link. He mustn't even think there is something going on. Use library pictures of the train but DO NOT put that on the screen. That will flag up a change to Kourash. He is used to seeing live streaming 24-7. Let's keep up that pretence."

"But that's lying to the British public," a lone voice protested.

The Prime Minister's press secretary shot the hapless man a withering look. "It's a damn sight better than having the deaths of hostages on your conscience."

"And nothing new," muttered another reporter.

After that, there was no more dissention and the press conference broke up.

Major Blunt stood in the shadows of the Northern Rail repair shed, watching Captain Thomas brief his men.

"Right lads, everything is ready. I'd like to thank you for all your hard work over the last few days, training, training and training yet again. But believe me, it'll pay off tonight. Just one last thing. I've had word from Ribblehead railway station. The hostages know you're coming. There is an army lad on the train, so they should have been told that we're coming in. Standard procedure is for them to lie on the floor, under the seats if possible, so keep the firing line up above the seats. Right?"

"Yes, sir," they called in unison.

"Very well. Do your best. Do your duty and bring home the hostages alive. We are the best there is. Your country needs you to send a short, sharp message to any terrorists out there thinking of pulling a similar stunt. Don't fuck with the British. Yes?"

"Yes, sir!"

"You all have your roles, you know what to do, so go and do it and God speed."

God speed, indeed, thought Blunt. The British public would never know the identities of the SAS men who would be tomorrow's heroes. Only that they were part of an elite force specially trained in rescue tactics. Once the job was done, they'd be whisked away, their faces never seen by anyone, not even those who they were rescuing. Debriefing would take place back at their base in Hereford.

A communications monitoring module had been set up in the shed, where live pictures would be beamed to Blunt via satellite, as well as to the Prime Minister, who would be watching with members of COBRA and to the centre at Ribblehead station. Once it was all over and the Prime Minister had congratulated Major Blunt and his team, they would disappear into the night. Until the next time.

Billy had never seen the hostages this dejected. It wasn't just the strain of still being held captive on the train for nearly 72 hours. As if that wasn't bad enough. But now they'd had to contend with the messages from their families.

One by one Kourash had brought them into the driver's cab, where his laptop was connected to the satellite link. He'd shown them their families on television, pleading with the Government to accede to Kourash's demands, so that their loved ones could be freed. Just like the prisoners in Bagram.

It was the cruellest thing Kourash could have done

to them. Hazel cried, her hands, as always, around her belly, protecting her unborn child. The sight of her dishevelled husband too much for her. Emma had lost it completely, returning from the cab, sobbing uncontrollably, needing to be helped back to her seat.

"It's made it so real," she whispered, "seeing my mum on television like that. I've never seen her so upset. I miss her so much. I want to go home, Billy. When can we go home?"

And that was the trouble. By confronting the hostages with the reality that their families were waiting on the 'outside' for their safe return, Kourash had bulldozed through their thin emotional shields, flaying them into submission. God only knew what it was doing to Charlie. That was Billy's biggest fear. The lad had lost his father, was separated from his mother and had just now been confronted by the sight of her crying into the camera. Her heartache clear for all to see. It was too much for the 11 year old and it had broken him. He was enfolded in Peggy's arms, no longer screaming and crying, but mute. His eyes dull and unseeing. The shock making him introverted and rendering him no more capable of coherent thought than a marble statue.

Billy was the last one to be called into the driver's cab, to be confronted by Kourash.

"So, Billy boy," Kourash mocked. "There doesn't seem to be anyone waiting for you to return home. No mobile phone and seemingly no family. Doesn't that strike you as odd?"

"No."

"Why no phone, Billy?"

"I told you before, I lost it."

"When?"

"Must have been somewhere on Carlisle station. After I boarded the train I realised it was missing, but there was nothing I could do about it by then."

"Yeah, right," Kourash sneered. "So what about your parents? Won't they be worried about you?"

"That would be difficult, they're dead," Billy kept his face impassive.

"No other family then? No brothers, sisters?"

"Only child of only children, before you start asking about aunts and uncles and cousins."

"You know something, Billy?" Kourash asked, then answered his own question. "I don't believe a word you're saying."

Billy just shrugged in reply, before being booted out of the driver's cab. Literally.

21:00 hours

Kourash had just announced, or rather gloated, Billy decided, that the British Government had agreed to his demands and that by 9 am tomorrow morning he would have confirmation that his brother was on the list of those prisoners to be released from Bagram Detention Centre. That meant they would be able to go home. In a few day's time. He'd strutted up and down the carriage, chest puffed out, black curls swinging, AK47 strapped across his chest. Give him a beret and he would have been perfect as a Ché Guevara lookalike, Billy thought.

His announcement hadn't done much to lift the hostage's morale. The thought of more agonising days trapped in the confines of the carriage, a hammer blow.

"I don't think I'll make it," Hazel whispered when Kourash had gone.

"I don't think Charlie will make it, either," said Peggy, who still had Charlie with her. She'd persuaded him to lie across a seat with his head in her lap. She was stroking his hair as he slept, thumb in mouth.

Billy made a snap decision and said, "It's alright, we won't have to wait that long."

"What?" Mick said. "Please God, are they coming?"

"Yes," confirmed Billy. "Tonight, or rather tomorrow morning."

This whispered announcement brought more tears, but with them watery smiles.

"So, we must carry on as normal. The hijackers mustn't know."

Billy stole a glance at the two men watching them. But they were more interested in jabbering to each other and eating. Cramming food into their mouths with their fingers, in-between sentences. It was disgusting and Billy looked away.

"So," he continued, "I can't come round and wake you all up, it would look suspicious and we must maintain the element of surprise. So if you do manage to sleep..."

"Fat chance," interrupted Mick.

"Then as soon as you are woken by the noise, you must immediately get on the floor and roll under a seat, if possible," Billy finished.

"What's it going to be like?" Peggy wanted to know.

"It will be very loud, very confusing, very scary. There'll be lots of deliberate shouting, to add to the confusion. Just get on the floor and stay where you are until either I or a member of the special forces come to get you."

"How will I know it's a member of the forces?" asked Emma. "For all I know in the darkness and confusion, it could be Kourash coming to get me!" Her hysteria, never far from the surface, began to bubble up again.

"They'll have guns," replied Billy, trying to calm her down.

"So do the hijackers," Mick pointed out.

"Oh yes, sorry," Billy smiled. "They'll have full body armour on and more than likely gas masks and or night vision goggles. Does that help?"

"Yes, thanks, Billy," murmured Emma. She was sitting on a seat, feet up, clasping her knees, a position she'd stayed in since seeing her mother on television. "I just want to go home," she whimpered. "I've had enough. I can't take anymore…"

As Hazel moved seats to comfort her, Billy tried to get morale up. "Right we need to keep things as normal as possible. Who's up for beating me at a game of cards?"

21:00 hours

The drum, drum, of the wheels against the tracks was the signal Captain Thomas had been waiting for. The food drop was underway. The Northern Rail pick-up truck was still in service, delivering an evening meal and other supplies to the hijackers and hostages. Now a well practiced routine, after the debacle of the first run when Potts had been shot.

He and his men were hidden in a clump of trees just shy of the viaduct. They had successfully completed the first part of the mission, to gain this position without being seen. The second part was trickier. Under the cover of the trees they had to inch their way to the edge of the valley. Then break cover and run to the bottom of the first set of arches, where they would be once again be invisible to anyone on look-out duty at the end of the train. The fact that Kourash had blown up the second carriage helped Thomas and his men. The hijackers no longer had a clear line of sight along the track. The twisted hulk of metal, plastic and fabric acting as a barrier and limiting their view.

Two clicks on the radio was the signal. Thomas waited until the pick-up truck was in place before he sent the two clicks. The noise of unloading the supplies and chattering voices would mask any sound they would inadvertently make. Two by two, his men followed him. Traversing the slope as quickly and quietly as possible. Rendezvousing at the bottom of the first arch. The huge grey granite blocks of the arch towered above them. A great hulking structure looking impossibly high and smooth.

Once all his men were in place, Thomas waited and again listened, making sure there was still distracting noise from the supply drop. Hearing the anticipated melee of voices, he sent one click, signalling that it was time for them to start moving along the arches. In teams of two men they ran forward, ducking back under the shelter of the viaduct and pausing before moving forward once again, until they were all in position on both sides of the arches, directly under the train.

The third part of the plan involved them waiting in the darkness. Dressed all in black with balaclavas on, the only part of their faces visible were eyes and mouths. Melting into the blackness and shadows of the viaduct they sat, backs against the rock. It was thought it was best to sit, rather than their usual camouflage waiting position of lying down. The arches themselves would act as better cover than the rock and bare ground ever could.

Once everyone was in place Captain Thomas allowed himself to relax. Just a little. For there was still much work to be done.

Billy moved amongst the hostages, handing out the Styrofoam cups of hot soup, urging his fellow hostages to drink, as they all needed to keep their strength up.

Sandwiches had also been provided, but they were proving too much for some of them. The twin feelings of fear and anticipation of the rescue, joining forces to close up throats, making swallowing lumps of bread pretty much an impossibility.

Charlie was being persuaded to drink some soup by his surrogate mother, Peggy. Helping Charlie was helping her, she'd confided to Billy earlier. Looking after him, as she looked after her children at home, had given her an anchor in the sea of unreality they'd found themselves drifting in. Billy said that was good. Two lonely people helping each other out. Charlie's vulnerability bringing out the mothering instinct in Peggy and Peggy's experience of motherhood helping Charlie through this, until he could be re-united with his own mother.

Emma was definitely at breaking point, Billy realised as he helped her lift the cup of nourishment to her lips.

"Come on, Emma. Just try a little sip," he urged as she turned her blank stare towards him. "Not much longer now, love. You'll be going home soon."

Emma obeyed his instruction, but he wasn't sure she was really listening to him. Rather listening to some inner voice that ebbed and flowed within her. Over the last few hours she had frequently cried and mumbled to herself, her book long since discarded. Unable to interact with her fellow passengers, she'd sat huddled in a corner, alone.

"You okay, Mick?" Billy turned his attention to the only other male passenger left on the train.

"Right as rain, Billy," he said and he smacked his lips appreciatively at the soup. "Nice this," he said. "You should have some as well, lad."

"Come on, Billy," Hazel joined in. "Sit here with us

and try and eat something."

Billy dropped into a seat next to Mick and collected some soup from Hazel. As he raised it to his lips the rain started. The soft misty drizzle giving way to a sudden downpour.

"Typical English weather," remarked Mick, raising his voice slightly over the drumming of the drops on the roof.

"Good for ducks," Hazel said.

"And special forces," chipped in Billy and they shared a complicit smile.

Crane arrived back at the station from his duty on the pick-up truck. As he finished unloading some rubbish they'd collected, Kean asked, "All well?"

"Yes, as far as I can tell. Although this time Kourash kept the hostages well out of the way, so I wasn't able to see any of them."

"How did Kourash seem?"

"Quite chirpy. But then he would be, he thinks he's going to get a list tomorrow morning of the names of prisoners going to be released from Bagram."

"Bloody idiot." Keane said.

"Amen to that," agreed Crane. "We just need to get through the next few hours, without Kourash doing anything stupid."

"I think we'll be okay. There is often a lull in activities once we get to about Day Two or Three."

"Why?" Crane wanted to know.

"It's a bit like the boredom sets in. Everyone, hijackers and hostages alike, become resigned to their fate and hunker down for the long haul. If we were to let things run, instead of going in tonight, then I would anticipate things would pick-up again tomorrow. It depends on the man in charge, really. Depends when the frustration boils over and chaos ensues."

"Which it would definitely do if Kourash realised there was no list of prisoners to be released. And that his brother would never be on the list, even if there was one."

"Exactly."

"In that case, thank God we're going in tonight," Crane once again evoking the name of the higher being everyone was praying to. Not only the families of the hostages, but those of the hijackers. All praying for a swift end to the siege. But what outcome would those prayers bring? Death and destruction was a dead cert. But who's death? Crane knew how he was feeling about Billy and that was bad enough. How would he feel if it was Tina in there? His son? A thought too horrible to contemplate without a crutch, so he pulled a packet of cigarettes out of his pocket.

Day Four
04:00 hours

Billy sneaked a peek at the time. It was 04:00 by his watch, but of course that could be wrong, he hadn't had anything to check it against for days. He desperately wanted to wake his fellow hostages, but that could wake the hijackers. And he needed them asleep...

Jesus Christ!

Jets screamed above his head, swooping down, flying low over the carriage. It had started. Billy slid off his seat to his knees and grabbed Emma, whom he considered to be the most vulnerable, pulling her to the ground with him. As she hit the floor with a thud, she screamed, but Billy ignored her protestations and rolled her under the seat.

Billy tried to shout to Mick, Hazel and Peggy, but his voice was useless above the noise of the aircraft. But he needn't have worried, they had already reacted instinctively and were dropping to the floor.

He looked around the seat he was squatting behind to see the two hijackers jabbering, looking around, pointing their guns at the roof.

"Shoot!" screamed Kourash as he burst through the

door from the driver's cab.

His men obeyed his order and began peppering the ceiling with bullets.

"Not up there, shoot the hostages you fools!"

As the AK47's turned towards the carriage seats, Billy ducked back behind his fragile barrier. But they only got a few rounds off before the demons of hell broke through into the carriage. And from somewhere, God knows where, Billy was that disoriented, a couple of machine guns barked into the night.

Windows smashed and stun grenades were thrown in. The flashes searing across Billy's eyes as he hadn't managed to close them in time. Then the smoke grenades peppered the floor and began billowing thick fog through the carriage. After a few seconds Billy could no longer see the hijackers. The smoke got in his throat and as he coughed he tugged at his shirt and tried to pull it up over his nose and mouth.

The hijackers began firing wildly and bullets streamed from their guns, cutting through the smoke, trying to find a target. Any target. Bullets thumped into the back of seats, glanced off the floor, pinged off the roof. A deadly, unpredictable, small lump of metal, flying through the air at hundreds of miles per hour.

Billy got ready to fling himself over to Emma, across the aisle, just a few feet away. Mick was looking after Hazel and Peggy was shielding Charlie's body with her own. As Billy tensed his body and pushed off, like a sprinter from the blocks, Kourash barrelled into him, knocking him out of the way. Billy scrabbled and crabbed trying to turn himself around to go back up the carriage, but he was too late. Kourash had reached Emma.

Kourash pulled her to her feet, put a gun to her head

and bent down to shout something in her ear. Whatever it was, she looked around and started screaming. A scream that was quickly extinguished by Kourash's hand over her mouth. He dragged her along and they both went backwards up the carriage towards the driver's cab door. At least Kourash's fellow hijackers had the sense to stop firing, while their leader moved along the carriage. Just as he disappeared into the fog, there was a dull thud, followed by a gust of damp air. The carriage doors had been blown off. Black coated figures flung themselves through the now open doors. The shouting was merciless.

"On the floor. Get down now. Drop your weapon. Down, I said get down!"

Over and over again. Accompanied by short bursts of gun-fire. Highly targeted. Highly deadly.

Billy did as he was told. No need for him to be a hero. There were lots of them on the train now. He felt a hand on his back and turned to see what was clearly a member of the special forces holding up a thumb. Checking he was alright. Billy nodded but then motioned the man down. Once his mouth was near the soldier's ear Billy yelled out his concern for Emma.

"A hostage taken. Drivers cab. Up there," and he pointed to where he knew the door was, even though he still couldn't see it.

A further thumbs up and the soldier moved away, looking as though he were mumbling to himself but no doubt saying something into his communications equipment.

It only took a few seconds more, a few rounds of bullets, a few screams, before Billy heard the soldiers shout, "Clear."

It might be clear in the carriage, but not up in the

driver's cab. Billy clambered to his feet, straining to get to the cab, wanting to know about Emma. But he ran into the brick wall that was one of his rescuers.

"Get down. This carriage may be clear but the train isn't secure. Do as you're told and help the others." At least Billy thought that was the gist of what the man was saying. His ears were still ringing from the stun grenades, gun fire and shouting.

Reluctantly he returned to the hostage's vulnerable hiding places to check everyone else was alright.

Mick was grinning, his arms still around Hazel. "Just like the pictures, eh lad!" he managed to shout.

"Hazel?" Billy shouted and gave a questioning thumbs up, to which he received a nod in reply.

Peggy was holding a wailing Charlie, all the while rocking him, but the boy didn't look like he was going to stop screaming anytime soon.

A soldier arrived like a mirage seen through the heat of the desert.

"We have to get you out. Follow me," and he and Billy pushed, pulled and cajoled the others up onto their feet and they made their way unsteadily to the door, where more rescuers were waiting to help them off the train.

Mick was the last one to leave. He'd let go of Hazel, who'd been picked up by a soldier and carried off. But he was still sitting down. Billy gestured for him to hurry up. But Mick still didn't move.

Billy bent down to help him and found he had to pull Mick up off the floor. All his earlier bravado gone. His blustering was just bluff. And that bluff had been called. Holding a shivering, shaking Mick upright he passed him to the next soldier, who bundled him down the carriage towards the blown off door.

Billy was supposed to follow, but went in the opposite direction. Towards the driver's cab.

"Oy," a voice called. "Out. Now."

"No," shouted Billy. "I'm not leaving her."

"Look, mate," someone grabbed hold of him and hissed in his ear. "There are still bombs on board. Everyone off."

"I'm not everyone." Billy could shout as loudly as any other soldier. "I'm army and I'm staying."

"Fucking hell. Well it's your funeral," the man said and tossed Billy a discarded weapon.

04:05 hours

"Situation report," Major Blunt asked of Captain Thomas.

"In the carriage, four hijackers killed, four hostages disembarked, one hostage, army lad, insisting on staying. In the cab believe two hijackers and one hostage."

"Ask that army lad, is there a bomb in the cab."

After a short pause, "Yes, sir," came the voice of the nearest member of Thomas' team to Billy. "In the form of a bicycle."

"Very well. Await further orders."

Major Blunt radioed the two hovering attack helicopters that had been responsible for the machine gun fire earlier. They were hovering over either side of the train, a hundred yards or so above it.

"Move into position. Front cab. Confirm you can see two hijackers and one hostage."

"Roger that," came the reply and on his satellite image Blunt could just make out faint lights from instruments inside the helicopter as they moved into position, one at either side of the train, the helicopters dropping level with the driver's cab door. He knew that on each chopper was a sniper, poised by the open door, wearing heat vision goggles. Night vision goggles wouldn't have been any good. The hijackers had long since put a film coating on the windows, so they could see out and no one could see in. But no one could hide from heat seeking goggles. The hijackers would show up as red figures, brandishing red weapons, if those weapons had recently been fired. Which they would have been.

"What can you see?" he asked the snipers.

"One hijacker my side, looking out of the window, machine gun in hand, raised in the air," said sniper number one.

"One hijacker holding a hostage as a shield, by the door, on my side, looks like a hand gun at hostage's head," said sniper number two. "Hostage facing the window. Hijacker behind."

"Have you a clear shot?"

"Affirmative, clear head shot," said one.

"Not yet," said two.

"Clear head shot," said one.

"Still no," said two.

"Still clear head shot," said one.

"Still.....affirmative, clear shot," confirmed two.

"Take it."

Blunt kept his eyes on the satellite picture, seeing two simultaneous flashes. One from each helicopter.

"Target down," said sniper one.

Blunt held his breath.

"Target down, hostage safe," said sniper two.

"Driver's cab clear. Repeat driver's cab clear," Blunt said to his team. "Well done everyone."

His voice was cold and calm and detached. But he exhaled a thankful breath as he removed his headset.

Billy could hear the helicopters turn away, the sound of their blades disappearing into the distance. Soldiers in front of him fumbled with something on the driver's cab door and the others started fumbling at their goggles, pulling them off and turning on torch lights attached to their uniforms.

"Down!" someone shouted and every man obeyed. The blast of the door lock being blown out seemed faint by comparison to the earlier cacophony.

"Emma!" Billy shouted and pushed through the doorway, an adrenaline surge making him stronger, quicker to react than the others and he reached her before them. He saw two hijackers, one by each door. Both dead, both with bullet wounds in their heads. Emma was lying on top of Kourash, who had a hand gun in his hand and Billy realised what had happened. Kourash had tried to use Emma as a human shield. So in the end Kourash couldn't bring himself to blow up the train, Billy realised. He had been shown up for the coward he was. Not even brave enough to be a suicide bomber. But a coward who killed people who were no threat to him. Like Colin. Or, as in the case of Emma, hid behind a woman.

As someone turned a light towards Emma, Billy bent over her lifeless body, placing a finger on her neck. She appeared uninjured. There was no blood that Billy could see in the jerking lights, which were making him feel as if he was in a silent movie. Every move he made as though picked out by strobe lights. Emma was unconscious. She must have suffered a blow to the head, he surmised, as she fell out of Kourash's final, treacherous, embrace. The embrace that had started out as attraction all those days ago, ending up as hatred. Feeling a faint pulse under his finger, he shouted, "She's alive," and hoisted her up, cradling her in his arms.

"Here, mate," someone said and went to take Emma from him.

But Billy shook his head. It was his job to carry her off the train. His responsibility. It was the least he could do.

04:10 hours

Searchlights that had been placed on the roof of the pick-up truck, were illuminating the track and in the distance, the train. Crane had watched the start of the rescue mission from his position further back along the line. Seeing some things, but hearing everything. The rapid tattoo of gun-fire, the flash of the stun grenades, the tracers of the bullets fired and the sound of screaming. Male and female. Hostages? Hijackers? Difficult to tell in the confusion.

He was plugged into the communications system and so could hear Major Blunt and his team and as soon as the snipers confirmed the hijackers were down, Crane screamed at the driver to start the bloody engine and get a bloody move on.

In the pick-up truck's flat bed behind Crane, army doctors and nurses crouched down, encumbered by equipment bags. Stretchers had been loaded on board along with defibrillators, drips, medication, everything they would need to set up a make shift emergency triage right there on the tracks. They were well trained in coping with injuries in the theatre of war, but a train track was a first for all of them.

Crane heard the attack helicopters swoop away, to be replaced by rescue helicopters, their bright searchlights piercing the evil that had enveloped the train. An evil repelled by the brave SAS lads, who would disappear as quickly as they'd appeared.

As the pick-up truck lurched to a stop a couple of metres from the train, the medics scrambled off the back and ran around the sides of the truck towards the train, as stumbling towards them, came the first of the hostages, each assisted by a member of the special forces. In teams of two they ran, one doctor and one nurse, carrying a stretcher between them. All patients were to be stretchered off. No exceptions. God forbid they should be rescued from the train, just to fall off the track in the darkness and confusion and fall 100 feet to their deaths. They would be disorientated from the rescue, their vision compromised from the stun grenades and hearing deadened from the noise.

First to arrive was what appeared to be a rather oversized woman, but Crane quickly recognised the pregnant hostage, Hazel. As she was placed on the stretcher, she was screaming in pain and holding her swollen belly. She'd gone into labour. Not surprising. The medics quickly set up a drip, strapped her on the stretcher and signalled for the rescue harness from the first helicopter.

Poised for the call, it took no more than a couple of heartbeats for the harness to appear and with it a member of the flight team. Inching down towards the track in a well practiced routine. Hazel would be transferred directly to Leeds hospital, where her husband was waiting for her. Indeed all of the hostages' families would be there. They had been woken up at 02:00 hours, told of the rescue mission and taken to the rendezvous point in the hospital. Apart from Billy's that was. His parents were still blissfully unaware that their son was on the train.

Then a shivering woman and a hysterical boy appeared, were treated and evacuated, followed by a man who, when his rescuer let him go, promptly fell to the tracks.

Crane watched all of this through the windscreen of the pick-up truck, obeying orders to stay out of the way. He watched the four hostages being treated and airlifted to safety, wondering all the time where the final two were. Feet itching to leave the truck, hands tapping on the dashboard, knees bobbing up and down.

And then Crane saw it. Saw what was for him the iconic image of the conclusion to the hijack. Billy emerging from the darkness and the fog that still clung to the wreck of the train, carrying Emma in his arms. Walking into the light. Walking to safety.

06:00 hours

Already the television was full of it. The rescue. Calls of 'hurrah' for the brave lads who had stormed the train and rescued the six hostages, without any casualties. Crane noticed that the news programmes carefully avoided information about the dead hijackers. Just kept going on about mission accomplished with no loss of life.

Crane watched the television placed high up on the wall of the waiting room in the hospital. Also waiting for Billy was Diane Chambers. Having been told of the blossoming relationship between the two young people by Harry, Crane had decided to call her after the rescue and suggested she meet him at the hospital, so she could see Billy. Unless she had something better to do, that was. Diane had said not on your bloody life.

Harry, meanwhile, was pushing Diane for an editorial piece, a human story behind the tragedy. He remained at the rescue site, to write about the aftermath of the rescue. For that he needed to see the remains of the train in daylight. So whilst waiting for Billy, she was scribbling away furiously one minute, then chewing her nails and gazing into space another.

She put her pad and pen down and stood up. "How much longer, Crane?" she asked and began pacing.

"Shouldn't be too long, he's been in there an hour already. He seems alright, but they just wanted to double check. Apparently he's a bit dehydrated, as they all are, but that's to be expected. Anyway when he does come out, you won't have long, I have to take him for debriefing. You do understand don't you?"

"Understand what?"

They turned at the sound of Billy's voice. There he was. Still dressed in his now somewhat overly distressed jeans and boots, his leather jacket slung over his shoulder.

"Billy!" Diane squeaked, then went bright red and began studying her shoes.

Smiling Crane took the two strides needed to meet Billy in the doorway. "Good to see you, lad," he said. And then coughed when nothing else would come out. Holding out his hand he found his voice and said, "Fucking good job you did in there," and shook Billy's hand that seemed far steadier than his own. "Oh bollocks," Crane said and grabbed Billy, hugging him and clapping in him on the back.

"Good to be back, boss," smiled Billy as they parted. "Sorry I'm a bit late," and they both laughed, as Billy had been due to arrive back at Aldershot Barracks three days ago.

Crane, for once deciding to be subtle, moved away, so Diane could come forward and he pointedly looked at the television.

"Hope you haven't forgotten that we've a date arranged for Friday night," she said. "I was beginning to think you were going to stand me up."

"I've never been known to miss a date with a

beautiful woman in my life, and I don't intend to start now," he told her and Crane saw Billy bend to kiss Diane out of the corner of his eye.

At Crane's cough, Billy, rather reluctantly it seemed, pulled himself away from Diane, his hand lingering on her arm and he said to her, "Sorry got to go for debriefing. See you Friday?"

"Just try and stop me...." she said and Crane pushed Billy out of the door and away from the grinning girl.

"Date eh?" he teased. "With Diane Chambers?"

"Yeah, well," Billy smiled, "We promised each other we wouldn't talk about our jobs, if we were to see each other."

"And how's that working out?"

"Pretty bloody well, wouldn't you agree, boss?"

"Yes I would, Billy," Crane said nodding. "Yes I would."

Be Careful What You Pray For
An editorial piece by our investigative reporter,
Diane Chambers,
who spent four days covering the hijack for the
Daily Record and the Aldershot News

The prayers of a nation were answered yesterday when members of the armed forces liberated the hostages. The prayers were for a successful end to the hijack. Successful in terms of the hostages being led out alive, that was. And that's exactly what happened. Pretty damn good result, I hear you say.

But that got me thinking. What about the prayers of the families who prayed to Allah for the safe return of their boys? The families of the hijackers. There was no liberation for those young men. No grand exit, smiling and waving to the press as they came out of Leeds hospital. Those families won't be taking their sons home in a wheelchair or on crutches. No. They will be taking their boys home in coffins.

One set of prayers answered. One not. Or maybe looking at it a different way, one set of prayers answered, but at what price? I can only hope that in prayers led by the Archbishop of Canterbury and other religious leaders, when they give thanks to their God, they take a moment to realise what it has meant for them to have their prayers answered. It meant that others had to die.

So maybe, just maybe, it would be appropriate for all those vicars and priests taking Sunday services this weekend, to acknowledge, to recognise, that in order for the hostages to survive, the hijackers gave their lives. Young men. The eldest just 26 years old. With lives to live and dreams to dream. With families that cared for them. Mothers that gave birth to them. Fathers who taught them. Brothers who played with them.

Now don't get me wrong, I'm not condoning their actions. I believe the radicalisation of young Muslim men is a terrible thing, that begats terrible things. And anyway what exactly did they accomplish? I guess a few million more people know about Bagram Detention Centre in Afghanistan. But that's all. They didn't stop the unlawful detention. They didn't manage to get anyone released. But at least they died for their cause, didn't they? In that case I hope that brings some comfort to their grieving families. But I doubt it. I think they'd rather have their sons back with them. Alive. Don't you? Instead of celebrations, they will hold funerals. Instead of life, they got death. Instead of a future, only tears.

Truman Capote puts it far better than I ever could.

"More tears are shed over answered prayers, than unanswered ones."

So during this weekend of celebration, as we shed the occasional tear of joy, let us not forget those who are crying many more tears of sadness, because our prayers were answered.

Prologue

Sgt Billy Williams returned to his Royal Military Police Unit at Aldershot Garrison, occasionally haunted by images of Emma consorting with Kourash, although he never regretted covering it up. His parent's were never told that he'd been on the train. He managed to keep his date with Diane Chambers.

Emma Harrison survived her head wound, completed her English Degree and wrote a true crime account of the hijacking. It was not as successful as In Cold Blood. She joined the Prison Service from University, on a fast track graduate program. After three years she became Junior Governor at Reading Young Offenders Institute (HMYOI) as deputy head of offender management.

Mick Smith never drove a train again, nor did he ever work again and took early retirement on health grounds.

Hazel Mountford was successfully delivered of a baby boy, albeit rather earlier than expected. She named him Billy. Instead of returning to work at her local supermarket after her maternity leave, she decided to stay at home to look after her baby.

Colin Appleton died of a heart attack on the rescue helicopter. Miraculously he wasn't shot during his rescue.

Charlie Thornton was re-united with his mother, Constance, at the end of the siege. He underwent years of counselling and Constance dedicated her life to raising him. She never re-married after her husband was killed during the hijack.

Peggy Richards resigned from Northern Rail, preferring to remain at home with her family. She never travelled on public transport again.

*****

Read on for an excerpt of Past Judgment, the new mystery series featuring Emma Harrison from Hijack and Sgt Billy Williams.

Past Judgment
Author Note

Her Majesty's Young Offenders Institute (HMYOI) in Reading is no longer a working institute. However, the building is still there and plans are being considered by Reading Council to turn it into a hotel and leisure complex.

The prison has a long and rich history and its most notable prisoner was Oscar Wilde, who wrote the Ballad of Reading Goal, based on his incarceration there.

I worked as a teacher in the Education Department at Reading HMYOI, teaching a range of subjects including English, Maths, Computer Skills, Art and, rather badly, Cookery. I loved my time at Reading and also at other nearby prisons, where I did supply teaching. My family has experience in prison education. My father was Deputy Chief Education Officer for Prisons and Borstals in England and Wales in the 1970's and 1980's and my mother taught at Reading Prison and Broadmoor. Both had the dubious pleasure of meeting some of Britain's most notorious prisoners.

Whilst the Judgment series may draw on our experiences from time to time, all characters and events are fictitious. Although I try and be true to policies and procedures, this is a work of fiction. Therefore, all mistakes are my own.

About Past Judgment

The past has a way of catching up with you....

At least it does for Emma Harrison, newly appointed assistant governor for inmate welfare at Reading Young Offender's Institute and for Leroy Carter, a prisoner who has been convicted of murder. When the prison van taking Leroy to Dartmoor crashes and he escapes, he's hell-bent on proving his innocence.

Leroy and the original detectives on his case, have to face the past head on. But so does Emma, when a fellow passenger from the train hijack three years earlier walks back into her life.

Can Leroy prove his innocence? And has Emma exorcised the ghosts from her past?

1
Present day...

The prison transport vehicle Leroy was expected to climb into loomed into view. It was very large and very white and would carry him away from Reading Young Offenders Institute. From the security of all things known. His well practiced and comfortable routine. His cell mate, John. His courses in the Education Block. And, of course, Emma. Or rather Miss Harrison. He shrank back. Fearful. Unwilling to get into the claustrophobic cell he would be locked in. He turned slightly as if to run away, but the prison escort officer he was handcuffed to wasn't having any of it.

"Come on, lad. Leroy isn't it? In you go, it's not that bad when you get in there."

Leroy had to disagree with that one and wondered if the escort had ever had to travel in one of those 'cells' for any length of time.

"But..."

"No buts, in you go," and Leroy took one last deep breath of fresh air before he and his three travelling companions were pushed and pulled into the vehicle as though they were no more than cattle being herded into a milking shed or an abattoir. As Leroy climbed the two steps into the transport, he was told to stop opposite the second cubicle on his left. When he was told to get in it, Leroy looked at the escort then at the cubicle and wondered how the hell he was supposed to do that. There was very little room in the narrow space to even turn around. Especially for someone as tall and gangly as he was. Standing at over six foot, but without the bulk and muscle to make him intimidating, Leroy had taken to stooping over slightly. A posture that screamed leave me alone, I'm trying to make myself small so as not to be noticed.

"Back in, then I'll close the door and you can hold out your hands through the space in the bars," the exasperated officer told him. "Then I'll un-cuff you and you can turn and sit down."

Leroy managed to do as he was told as the door was banged shut. Then locked. Breathing deeply to try and stop the rush of claustrophobia from his brain flooding through his body, he looked out of the window. Glad for the small glimpse of the world outside. Focusing on the window, he tried to block out the noises of the back door being slammed and locked and then the cab doors being opened and closed. As the rumble of the diesel engine started its soundtrack to their journey, the van left Reading HMYOI, rumbling along the urban roads on its way to the motorway.

As they started their creaky, bumpy journey, Leroy's fellow prisoners made their feelings known. At the top of their voices. From abuse hurled at the escort officers and each other, to sexual references tossed in the direction of any woman unlucky enough to be passing by. They seemed to have an opinion on everything and everyone. Leroy added an extra layer on top of his claustrophobia. Fear. He was straight out scared of his fellow travellers. He hoped this noise and abuse wasn't a sign of things to come at Dartmoor Prison. So far the whole experience wasn't a good start to his new life in a new prison. He shrunk away from the noise, trying to blot it out, pushing back into the seat and turning slightly, trying to keep his back to the other prisoners.

Once on the motorway, the gentle rumble of tyres on asphalt calmed Leroy and he was able to relax a little and inspect his surroundings. Not that it took very long. He was sat on a grey plastic seat in a space smaller than an old fashioned telephone box. But a Dr Who Tardis this wasn't. The space wasn't larger inside than it seemed on the outside. White plastic was everywhere, gouged with irreverent messages from previous occupants. There was nothing to read, nothing to occupy his mind and he sunk into a daze. He became drowsy and must have dozed off, for he was woken by a dramatic clap of thunder.

The view outside his aircraft-type window was obscured by dark heavy clouds. They looked full of the rain they seemed determined to dump on the road. He watched with mounting fascination as the big fat heavy rain drops began to fall. One, two, four, eight, sixteen... until they fell so fast Leroy couldn't count them anymore. The drops fell faster and harder, bouncing ankle high off the ground, their rapid tattoo drilling into his brain. A tattoo that became louder as the raindrops turned into hailstones, some as large as golf balls. They carpeted the road, turning it into a white, icy, highway to hell.

The van, unable to find purchase on the road, began to veer first one way and then the other and Leroy, with nothing to hold onto, put his arms out and placed his hands palm up on each wall. Wet with sweat, they simply slid off the plastic. As the van swerved, Leroy went with it, unable to do anything but ride the storm. He heard tyres squeal as the van slewed sideways. With a bang, the van hit an unseen object and fell over, sliding along the road as though it were still on its wheels, not on its side. Leroy was thrown out of his seat and ended up lying, face down on the side wall that had suddenly become the floor.

After several seconds of screeching metal grinding against the road and Leroy feeling like he was on fairground ride, the transport ground to a halt. For a moment all was still. The kind of pregnant pause found inside the eye of a tornado. The brief period of calm, before the world descended into chaos once again. The other prisoners all began shouting at once. Cursing the weather, the officers and the van. But underneath
their yells Leroy could hear something else. He tuned out the yelling from his fellow prisoners as best he could, concentrating on the underlying sound. He recognised it as water. Water that was gushing and gurgling. That's when Leroy realised the van must have fallen into a river. His fears were confirmed when he felt his trousers getting wet. Water was permeating the prison van, seeking out and finding the smallest of gaps. Unchecked. Leroy and his fellow prisoners couldn't get away. The cubicles, so small and narrow, meant they were unable to stand. The doors were locked so they were unable to escape. There was no sign of the escorts. And the water was rising.

You can purchase Past Judgment at Amazon:

Meet the Author

I do hope you've enjoyed Hijack. If so, perhaps you would be kind enough to post a review on Amazon. Reviews really do make all the difference to authors and it is great to get feedback from you, the reader.

If this is the first of my novels you've read, you may be interested in the other Sgt Major Crane books, following Tom Crane and DI Anderson as they take on the worst crimes committed in and around Aldershot Garrison. At the time of writing there are six Sgt Major Crane crime thrillers. In order, they are: Steps to Heaven, 40 Days 40 Nights, Honour Bound, Cordon of Lies, Regenerate and this one, Hijack.

Past Judgment is the first in a new series. It is a spin-off from the Sgt Major Crane novels and features Emma Harrison from Hijack and Sgt Billy Williams of the Special Investigations Branch of the Royal Military Police. At the time of writing the second book, Mortal Judgment has just been released. Look out for more adventures from Billy and Emma in the Judgment series in the near future.

All my books are available on Amazon.

You can keep in touch through my website http://www.wendycartmell.webs.com where you can sign up to join my mailing list and in return get a free ebook! Everyone who signs up gets a free copy of Who's Afraid Now (kindle or pdf) a 10,000 word story which is a prequel to Hijack. Let me know which format you'd like and I'll email it to you, as a bonus for signing up. I'm also on Twitter @wendycartmell and can be contacted directly by email at: w_cartmell@hotmail.com

Happy reading until the next time...

Printed in Great Britain
by Amazon